SUPER JAKE &
THE KING OF CHAOS

SUPER JAKE &
THE KING OF CHAOS

BY **NAOMI MILLINER**

RP|KIDS
PHILADELPHIA

Running Press Kids
Hachette Book Group
1290 Avenue of the Americas, New York, NY 10104
www.runningpress.com/rpkids
@RP_Kids

Printed in the United States of America

First Edition: May 2019

Published by Running Press Kids, an imprint of Perseus Books, LLC, a subsidiary of Hachette Book Group, Inc.
The Running Press Kids name and logo is a trademark of the Hachette Book Group.

The Hachette Speakers Bureau provides a wide range of authors for speaking events. To find out more, go to www.hachettespeakersbureau.com or call (866) 376-6591.

The publisher is not responsible for websites (or their content) that are not owned by the publisher.

Print book cover and interior design by Christopher Eads

Library of Congress Control Number: 2018945857

ISBNs: 978-0-7624-6615-3 (hardcover), 978-0-7624-6616-0 (ebook)

LSC-C

10   9   8   7   6   5   4   3   2   1

FOR JAKE,
ALL THE CHILDREN LIKE HIM,
AND THE PEOPLE WHO LOVE THEM.
·····♥·····

SUPER JAKE & THE KING OF CHAOS

CHAPTER ONE

It doesn't matter if my audience is made up of nine-year-old superheroes with plastic hammers and shields, or ninety-year-old great-grandparents with white hair and walkers. Everybody loves magic. Especially me.

I've been doing magic shows for more than a year now, since the beginning of fifth grade, and I love every second of it. Today's show is in a living room decorated with pink streamers and pink balloons for a dozen three-year-old girls. Princess Jasmine is poking Pocahontas; Belle is whacking Sleeping Beauty with a balloon; and Snow White is screaming for her mommy.

Welcome to my world.

The birthday girl, Jenny, is a blue-eyed blonde dressed as Cinderella (except for the pink ribbons in her hair). Since I always do my research ahead of time, I knew what her costume would be. So, the first question I ask the group is: "Have any of you heard of Cinderella?"

Jenny gives me a giant smile while the girls around her shriek, "Jenny is Cinderella!"

I act surprised. "Wow! No way!" More shrieks. "Anyone know what Cinderella left at the ball?"

"Her glass slipper!" Princess Jasmine shouts.

"Exactly. And I happen to have a glass slipper right here in my hat. Who wants to see it?"

The twelve girls squeal and rush toward me for a better view. I raise my wand, tap it over my sparkly black top hat, and pull out . . .

"SpongeBob!" The girl dressed like Belle giggles and points.

I turn to my seven-year-old brother, Freddy, who's busy eating candy from my stars-and-moons-covered box.

Mom "suggested" I make him my assistant a few months ago when summer started and he had nothing to do.

"Ethan, why don't you put Freddy in your act?" Mom had asked.

Faster than you can say "Abracadabra," I gave a dozen reasons why this was a terrible idea. My favorite was, "What if I accidentally saw him in half?" No loving parent could possibly argue with that, right?

The next day Freddy pranced into the living room wearing a top hat, black shirt and pants, and a red bowtie. The top hat practically covered his eyes and the bowtie was crooked. It was like staring at myself in a fun-house mirror, everything exaggerated and strange-looking.

"Doesn't he look wonderful?" Mom gushed.

"He certainly does." Dad smiled, then put his arm around Mom's waist, pulling her close.

I usually hate sappy stuff, but it was kind of nice seeing my parents like that. They used to be like that all the time . . . until Jake was born and Mom got nervous and Dad got sad and everything changed. I guess I got a little sappy, too, because I agreed to give Freddy a chance. Turns out, my act's a lot funnier now (though I'll never tell him that).

Jenny and her friends laugh as I glare at Freddy and say, "Give me that candy!"

It's all part of our routine.

He shuts the box. "What candy?" He opens the box again, and it's empty.

I take the box, wave my wand over the lid, and the candy's back. I promise the girls they'll get plenty of candy soon, then ask the birthday girl what her favorite color is.

As predicted, she says, "Pink!"

Freddy starts pulling plastic rings and bracelets from my

Sorcerer's Apprentice hat: red, blue, purple. As the girls dive for the jewelry, Freddy cries, "Hey, there's no pink here!"

"Are you sure?" I ask. "I know I had something pink. Where did it go?" I turn my back to the audience, pretend to search, then turn around, one hand on my stomach and one over my mouth.

"Ethan?" Freddy asks. "You look kinda funny. Are you okay?"

I shake my head and scrunch my face up like I'm gonna be sick. Then I open my mouth and pull out a forty-six-foot-long coil of pink paper. Jenny and her friends laugh until their faces are pinker than the paper.

The show's gone perfectly, and I feel great. Freddy and I finish with our usual crowd pleaser: a magic hat full of lollipops. After the girls grab all the candy they can hold, they follow their moms and dads to another room for cake, and Freddy tags along with them.

I toss the last few items into my magic bag, then join the others. As Jenny's mom lights the first candle, the doorbell rings. Since the candle lighting is in full swing, I offer to get the door.

I squeeze my way through a waist-high maze of cardboard crowns and glittery tiaras and open the front door to see my mom. And Jake.

My great mood vanishes, because I know what's going to happen. In two seconds flat, my tricks will be as forgotten as the candy wrappers in my hat. Everyone will stare at Jake and try to figure out what's wrong with him. And, if things go really badly, someone will say something dumb and Mom will start crying.

"I thought Dad was supposed to pick us up." *Without Jake.*

"I know. But I wanted to see the little girls all dressed up. Besides, it was a good excuse for Jake to wear his new shirt. Isn't it cute?" Mom leans over and kisses him on the forehead.

Jake's wearing a Cookie Monster shirt, silently taking in the action all around him through his turquoise-framed glasses.

"Hey, Jake." As I lean over his purple-and-green Kid Kart—a cross between a stroller and wheelchair that helps him sit up—and ruffle his soft curls, somebody tugs at my shirt: it's birthday-girl Jenny.

"Who's that?" she asks.

And, here we go. My shoulders tense and my stomach tightens. "My other brother, Jake." I look around the room, hoping no one else will come over.

"How old is he?"

"He'll be two soon."

"Hi!" Jenny waves at him.

Jake watches her with his usual calm expression, only she wants more. People always do. She waits for him to answer or at least wave back.

He doesn't. He won't.

She tries again. "Hello?"

Jake is silent.

"Are his ears okay?" Jenny asks.

I want to leave. Now. I don't even care about my pay. I look at my mom. "Y'know, I don't feel so good. Can we—"

"Jake's ears are fine," Mom tells her. "But his brain was hurt before he was born, so some things are hard for him. Like waving or saying hello."

I hate when she does that. Why can't she just say his hearing is fine and leave it at that?

Jenny stops waving, looks at Jake for a few seconds, and runs away. Typical. Sometimes people a lot older look like they want to run, too—like brain damage is contagious or something.

"Jakey!" Freddy flies over, pink frosting all over his face, and gives Jake a hug. "I like your new shirt. Are you a Cookie Monster?" He squeezes Jake's hands and Jake rewards him with a big open-mouthed grin.

I feel another tug on my shirt. Jenny's back, and there's something in her hand: a Sleeping Beauty Band-Aid.

She holds it out for me to see. "For Jake's hurt brain," she says.

Mom takes the Band-Aid. She presses her lips together and her forehead crinkles, and I can tell she's about to cry. I close my eyes, wishing I could disappear, like the candy in my trick box.

"Jakey likes Spider-Man better than Sleeping Beauty," I hear Freddy say.

I open my eyes.

Jenny cocks her head like a puppy. "How do you know? He doesn't talk."

"Sure he does," Freddy tells her. "You have to know how to listen." He grabs Jake's hand and helps him wave. "See? He says hi."

By now, Mom has pulled herself together. She bends over to give Jenny a hug and wishes her a happy birthday while I do a major exhale. I feel like Houdini—another narrow escape . . . for now.

CHAPTER TWO

Mornings are one of my least favorite things. And Monday mornings? They're worst of all—at least, if school is involved. Still, I'm awake and dressed, a comb halfway through my crazy curly hair before giving up. I flop back onto my bed and look up at posters of Harry Houdini, David Copperfield, and Magnus the Magnificent, my three favorite magicians.

"Ethan, you'll be late!" Mom yells from the kitchen.

I wonder if Mrs. Houdini or Mrs. Copperfield yelled at their sons, too.

I run to the kitchen and scarf down a bowl of cereal, half listening as Mom says something about another doctor's appointment after school.

She sighs. "Ethan, have you heard one word I said?"

"At least one," I tell her. "Maybe two, possibly even three." I drain the rest of my milk.

"Wise guy." Her face relaxes into a smile, which makes me smile, too.

I haul my backpack over my shoulders, grab my trumpet case, and race out the door. When I reach the corner, Betty the Crossing Guard gives me her usual greeting: "Hey, Ethan, how ya' doin'?"

"Monday. Middle school. Math. How 'bout you?"

"Monday. Middle-aged. Minor arthritis."

"I thought life got better once you're out of school."

"So did I." She laughs.

I complain about school, but it's not bad. Not *that* bad. Middle school was definitely an adjustment, though. After six years at the same elementary school, it was a little scary to go to McAuliffe Middle School—especially for me. Because it wasn't just a new school; it was a new school *with my dad*. (Also known as the assistant principal.)

The first week, I was so busy finding my way around and getting used to everything that I forgot Dad was there, too. Then all of a sudden, I'd see him standing in the office or walking around the lunchroom or talking to one of my teachers or classmates. It was pretty weird.

These days, I don't mind so much. It just means I have to be on my best behavior . . . all the time. Mom says this shouldn't be hard, since I'm, quote, "a pretty good kid . . . *most* of the time." That's my mom. She's hilarious.

My favorite classes are first period (band) and last period (English with Ms. Carlin), but the best part of the day is lunch with Brian Parker and Daniel Chen. Brian moved here a few years ago and we became friends right away, because we both loved superheroes and computer games (especially computer games *with* superheroes).

I've known Daniel since I was Jake's age, and even though we've been friends forever, we never run out of stuff to do or talk about. If I had a dollar for every time we laughed together, I'd have enough money to buy a trick rabbit hutch I've had my eyes on since April. Maybe even the rabbit, too.

Brian takes a final slurp of his soda and I pop the last pretzel in my mouth, while Daniel pulls out the phone his parents bought him when he started middle school.

I wish I had one, too. But with Dad being at my school all day, and school being just a few blocks from our house, my parents say I don't need one yet. It's been an ongoing debate the past few months, but whenever it's Mom and Dad versus me—let's just say, the odds are not in my favor.

"I almost forgot," Daniel says. "I was on the Internet this morning and saw this."

He passes his phone to me. There's a picture of a guy in a tux with a wand, some cards, and a flying dove. Underneath, in huge letters, it reads MAGIC FEST: ATLANTIC CITY, NEW JERSEY. JANUARY 19–21.

"It looks pretty cool," Daniel says. "There are strolling magicians, a store full of magic tricks, and a competition for junior magicians ages ten to thirteen. And you'll never guess what the grand prize is: meeting and performing with your hero Magnus the Magnificent."

"This is unbelievable!" I can't stop staring at the picture.

Daniel smiles. "Thought you might like it."

"Like it? This is the coolest, greatest thing I've ever seen! I've gotta go. And I've gotta win, and I've gotta meet Magnus."

Just then the bell rings, signaling that lunch is over. But my plans are just beginning. Unfortunately, I have to put them on hold and suffer through my least favorite, most dreaded class of all.

When I walk into the room, there are already ten math problems on the board. Our teacher is at her desk, probably plotting today's torture. Her name is Miss Wright, but I think of her as Miss Wrong, because nothing about her, or the entire class, is ever right. Especially my answers.

Least favorite teacher + least favorite subject = one unhappy me.

I've gotten through six problems before I start thinking about Magic Fest and Magnus. Then I start thinking about a stage name, which I'll need for my act.

I'll need an act, too.

Houdini called himself "Prince of Air," "King of Cards," "The Handcuff King," and, my favorite, "The Genius of Escape." Maybe I can be "The Genius of—"

"Ethan?"

Definitely not "The Genius of Math."

The second Miss Wright opens her mouth again, an alarm goes off and there's a fire drill.

When we finally get back inside, Miss Wright barely has time to give tonight's assignment before the bell rings. I jot it down, grab my backpack, and race to the door.

Her skinny arm shoots out, barring my way. "Ethan, I feel like you don't even try. I know you can do better."

"Sorry." I'm hoping that's enough, but then she gives me The Face. Her eyes get all big and her face goes all soft, and I know what's coming.

"How is everything at home?"

By "everything" she means Jake. Ever since she saw our family at the grocery store last month, Miss Wright's been trying to be extra nice to me. But I don't need her help or her pity. I don't need her feeling sorry for me or thinking that being Jake's big brother ruins my life or makes me mess up in math class.

Miss Wright is definitely wrong about everything.

"Everything's great." I flash a fake grin. She looks at me for another second then lets me go.

I get to English class right before the bell rings. Unlike Miss Wright, Ms. Carlin is my favorite teacher. The first day of school she had each of us write a list of our five favorite things to get to know us better—and she made a list, too. When she read hers aloud, it turned out we had both written stuffed crust pizza and University of Maryland basketball. Plus, the next day I was wearing my LEFTIES ARE ALWAYS RIGHT! T-shirt, and she said she has one exactly like it.

Today, the second I walk through the door, she pulls me aside. "Ethan, we have a new student joining us today. I was wondering if you could take him under your wing and help him acclimate to our class?"

"Sure, no problem." I scan the chairs for a new face and notice that Brian is sitting across the room, instead of his usual place next to me.

"The new student's name is Ned," Ms. Carlin continues. "He should be here any moment."

"Oh," I tell her. "I think he's in my gym class, too."

She smiles. "That makes it even better! Would you mind if he sits next to you?"

Before I can even answer, he walks in. It's him all right— he's kind of hard to miss. Not only does he have frizzy red hair and tons of freckles, but he's big. Really big.

Incredible Hulk big.

It's a good thing I'll be helping him out. I wouldn't want to be on his bad side.

Ms. Carlin hands him a copy of the play we're reading— Shakespeare's *A Midsummer Night's Dream*—and he follows me to our seats.

Since there are twenty-five (now twenty-six) kids in class, we share the big parts when we read it aloud. It's pretty fun. I play Puck, the troublemaker, for the last two acts. Ms. Carlin claims it's not typecasting.

I show Ned where we are in the play and ask if he likes Shakespeare.

He shrugs.

"Have you read any of his other plays?" I ask.

He shakes his head.

"What were you reading in your old school?"

"Nothing."

I remind myself that Hulk was never much of a talker either as we start reading the scene.

When the bell rings at 2:40, everyone rushes out of the classroom, and the building, except me. Since I walk home, sometimes I stay after school and return books to the shelves or help with other stuff Ms. Carlin needs. I know it sounds nerdy, but she really is nice. Kind of pretty, too. For a teacher.

"Excellent job today, Ethan," Ms. Carlin says. "You make a very convincing Puck."

"Thanks. I pretend I'm my little brother Freddy and that helps, because he always causes trouble."

As I shelve books alphabetically, we talk about this year's University of Maryland men's basketball team. The new season starts next month, and we're both excited about it. She told me that when she was a student there, she went to every game with her roommate. One time, when the game was really close, she shouted so much she lost her voice. But she says it was worth it.

It's nice to have a conversation without being interrupted all the time, like I am at home. By the time I finish, it's almost 3:00 p.m.

I take my time walking home, enjoying the crunch of orange and red leaves under my feet. I don't know about October anywhere else, but here in Maryland it's pretty awesome.

What's even more awesome is the idea of going to Magic Fest, especially the part about meeting Magnus the Magnificent! The excited part of me can't wait to tell Mom and Dad all about it; the smart part of me knows I can't just blurt it out. Timing is important when it comes to asking my parents for stuff. It's not like they're mean or anything—they just have a lot going on, so I try not to bug them too often.

I'm partway up our driveway when Mom comes rushing out of the house. Her face is redder than the fallen maple leaves. "Where have you been, Ethan? I told you to come straight home!"

Something tells me this is *not* the time to bring up Magic Fest.

She's pointing to the minivan, so I swerve and climb into the middle row. Jake is already buckled in his car seat. As I put on my seat belt, Freddy leans over from the back with a big grin on his face and sings, "You're in trouble!"

Mom jumps into the front seat, glaring at me in the rearview mirror. "I cannot *believe* you forgot we're getting flu shots today. I told you about it this morning during breakfast."

I'd rather face a roomful of math equations.

"It's just an immigration," Freddy-the-Know-It-All says.

"Immunization, idiot," I snap back.

Freddy leans forward as far as the seat belt lets him. "Mommy! Ethan called me—"

"Milkshakes after," Mom interrupts. "For whoever doesn't give me grief."

The rest of the trip is silent.

At the doctor's office, once we check in and are seated in Room Three, Mom asks who will go first. Freddy looks at me.

"No way," I tell him.

As we argue, Jake's favorite nurse joins us. "Hey there, Mr. Jake! You are looking mighty fine today!" she says.

While Jake and the nurse smile at each other, Freddy and I keep at it until I agree to go first.

"Too late." The nurse laughs. "Mr. Jake already got his. Didn't you, handsome?"

"All right, Jakey!" Freddy lifts one of Jake's hands and taps it against his own for a high five. "You didn't even cry."

The truth is, Jake never cries, even when he gets a shot. It's like he doesn't feel the needle. I don't know if that's good or bad but, like always, I squeeze his hands, smile, and say, "Good job, Jake."

CHAPTER THREE

Mom keeps her promise and gets milkshakes for Freddy and me, and a small one for her and Jake to share. When we get home, she puts a little on a spoon for Jake to try, but he wrinkles his nose the way he does when he doesn't like something.

"It's probably too cold for him," Mom says.

She's feeding Jake a bottle in the living room while Freddy slurps his shake and I read aloud the first chapter in *The Fires of Merlin* to everyone. Mom and I have been reading books out loud to each other since I was little, and T.A. Barron's Merlin Saga is one of our new favorites.

Mom and I used to do lots of stuff together, like play board games, learn card tricks, and make up funny lyrics to popular songs. And every other Sunday, she and I went to this fifties-style diner, just the two of us, while Dad and Freddy did some little kid thing. We'd split a grilled cheese sandwich, then order two desserts and share them.

We've gone back to the diner a few times with Jake, but it's not the same. Mom gets distracted fussing over him and half the time it feels like she's not listening to me at all.

But we still read together. Today we're starting the third book in the Lost Years of Merlin series. Our neighbor and "honorary big brother," Chris Todd, gave me paperbacks of all five books for my birthday and Hanukkah presents last year. Right now, we're at the part in the story where Merlin's almost done making a magical harp.

"E!" Dad calls from the kitchen door. "Want to give me a hand with these groceries?"

What I want is to keep reading, but the faster I help, the sooner I can get back to Merlin, so I race out the door to the carport.

Dad hands me a carton of diapers, stacks a box of baby food on top of that, and then grabs a bunch of bags and opens the door for us both.

We start putting away the groceries in the kitchen. "So, when's your next gig?" He squeezes milk and orange juice into our crowded fridge.

I kneel in front of the cabinets where Jake's food goes and sort jars of mushy fruit, veggies, and meat. I'm about to tell Dad about the pirate party I'm doing this Sunday when Mom calls out, "Ethan? Could you please get the thermometer? Jake feels hot to me."

I groan—at least, on the inside. We'll never get back to Merlin at this rate. I run down the hall and bring back the special thermometer Mom uses for Jake, pretty much every five minutes.

One of the things that's different about Jake is his temperature. Sometimes it gets really high, other times really low. It happens so often that Mom always carries a little battery-operated fan in her bag in case he gets too hot and a blanket in case he gets too cold.

I hand her the thermometer and she sticks it through Jake's shirt, under his arm. After about ten seconds, it goes nuts: *beep beepbeep, beep beepbeep, beep beepbeep*. When it sounds like that, I know it means trouble, even without Mom biting her lip like she always does when she worries. She reads the thermometer. "Hundred and two point eight."

She takes off Jake's shirt and Dad hurries to the bathroom to start running water in the tub.

"Should I get his juice cup or the fan?" I ask.

Mom shakes her head. "Not right now. Maybe after the bath."

"Are we taking Jakey to the hospital again?" Freddy asks.

"I hope not," Mom says.

The first time Jake's temperature got super high, we didn't

know what to do. It was really scary until Mom and Dad finally managed to cool him down with an ice-cold washcloth. And the first time we took Jake to the emergency room, we all were freaking out—except Dad, who seems to stay calm no matter what.

Now we're used to crazy temperatures and ER visits and the Kid Kart and everything else that comes with Jake. It's just the way life is.

"Can I do anything?" I ask. When Mom shakes her head and says, "Not right now," I'm secretly relieved. It's not that I don't want to help. But whenever Jake's temperature gets too high or low, Mom calls the pediatrician and the rest of us run around trying to help and everyone gets stressed out.

While Mom and Dad try to cool down Jake in the tub, I go to my room, shut the door, and head to my laptop. It's Mom's hand-me-down, and it's not very fast, but it's better than nothing—especially since I don't have a cell phone yet. (Did I mention that?)

I find the link to Magic Fest that Daniel showed me and start exploring the site. The more I see, the more excited I get. I click tabs for past Magic Fests and watch videos of other magicians my age performing on YouTube. I find a new interview with Magnus, then watch him perform some of my favorite tricks . . . for about the twentieth time.

"E?" Dad opens the door. I look up from the computer and glance at the window, noticing that the sky's turning pink and purple. "Looks like we're going to the ER after all."

I turn the computer off and grab my shoes.

"You and Freddy are staying here. If the ER is crowded, we could be there a while."

"That's okay. I want to go with you."

Before Dad says another word, my grandfather walks in. "Hey, buddy." When he pulls me in for a hug, I can smell the wintergreen Life Savers he always gives Freddy and me on his breath.

"Hey, Bubba. When did you get here?"

"Just now. Your mom called and Emma and I came right over." (It's funny how everyone calls her Emma now. It started because, when I was little, I couldn't pronounce Grandma, and somehow the name stuck. Luckily, she likes it.)

"Sam, let's go!" Mom yells from down the hall.

"Coming!" Dad calls back.

Freddy runs into my room, which is starting to feel very crowded. "Ethan, guess what? We're having French toast for supper!" he says, like it's the best thing ever. (Actually, Emma's French toast *is* the best thing ever, but that's beside the point.)

"We'll be back before you know it." Dad squeezes my

shoulder. We follow him down the hall to the front door. Jake is waiting patiently in Mom's arms, but she's biting her lip and jiggling her foot. Another thirty seconds and she might drive off without Dad.

I lean over and rub Jake's hands together at lightning speed and he smiles at me, even though his eyes are more closed than open.

"Can we *please* go?" The way Mom says it, it's not a question.

"Bye, Jakey." Freddy waves as Dad carries Jake out to the car. "Come back soon!"

But he doesn't.

I'm reading my favorite chapter of *Harry Potter and the Prisoner of Azkaban* when Freddy barges into my room in his stegosaurus pajamas. "Whatcha doin'?"

"What am *I* doing? What are *you* doing?" I check my clock: 10:35 p.m. "You were supposed to be asleep, like, two hours ago!"

"I'm doing a huge battle of dinosaurs versus *Star Wars*. I thought the *Star Wars* people would win because they've got lightsabers. But the dinosaurs were hungry, so they ate them."

I raise my eyebrows. "The lightsabers?"

"The people."

"Freddy, it's way past your bedtime. Emma and Bubba are gonna be mad if they see you're still awake."

"They both fell asleep watching TV." Freddy plops onto my bed. "When's Jakey coming home?" He's clutching Pita Rabbit (formerly known as Peter Rabbit, but after years of being squished flat . . . you get the idea). This can only mean one thing: Freddy's scared.

I want to say that they'll be home soon, only they left almost four hours ago. It's never taken this long before. I don't know how to answer, so I go with the next best thing: "Wanna see a new trick?"

Freddy's Eeyore look disappears. He sits up and grins at me. I turn my back on him and start setting up. "No peeking!" I look around to see him close his eyes and *then* cover them with his hands. He may be annoying, but at least he's honest.

A minute later I'm ready with a bunch of note cards lying facedown on the bed. "Okay, you can open your eyes now. Each card has a superhero on it. The last one you turn over will be your favorite."

"Captain America?"

"Yep. Now pick two, but don't turn them over."

I point to the nine identical note cards. He chooses two. I turn one over.

"Iron Man," he says.

I put that card aside and pick two more. "Okay, turn either one of these over." He picks one.

"Black Widow." He shakes his head.

We go through it a few more times, until Freddy reveals the final card.

"Captain America! Wow! That was awesome!" His smile is better than a whole roomful of applause. "Do it again!"

"Tomorrow. We can try it with *Star Wars* characters."

He grins. "I want Han Solo!"

"I'll see what I can do. Right now, it's time for bed."

"Just one more trick," he bargains, as usual.

I grab my trusty top hat and wand from my dresser, say, "Abracadabra," and pull out a miniature photograph of Freddy.

He laughs, but then his smile disappears. "Now do Jake."

"I don't have a small enough picture of him."

Freddy shakes his head. "Not a picture. I mean, make Jake appear. For real."

I want to say, "That's impossible," only something in his face won't let me.

"I'll try. Then to bed, okay?" We go to Jake's room and stand by the little bed with the Elmo sheets and Pooh mobile and stuffed Tweety and Bugs Bunny, but no Jake. I raise my wand over the empty bed and, feeling really stupid, shut my eyes and say, "Abracadabra!"

Nothing happens.

"Sorry. Guess I'm not a good enough magician."

Freddy-the-Believer says, "Try again, just in case." He stands there in his ridiculous pajamas, looking so hopeful.

I wave my wand in the air again . . . just in case. "Abracadabra!"

Still no Jake.

Freddy looks like a balloon someone stuck a needle in. I put my arm around his drooping shoulder and say, "Time for bed." I wait for him to argue, but he goes right to his room without a fight, which makes me feel like even more of a failure.

I knew the trick wouldn't work.

But I wish it had.

CHAPTER FOUR

Not even five minutes later, I hear the front door open. Freddy and I burst out of our rooms and race down the hall to see Mom and Dad . . . and Jake.

"You're back!" Freddy dances around.

I give Jake a welcome-home hug, even though he's asleep.

"What are you doing awake at this hour?" Mom asks.

I'm too busy yawning to answer.

"Never mind." She smiles, gives me a hug, and turns me in the direction of my room.

My head hits the pillow and I'm out in thirty seconds.

Next thing I know, the sun is shining through my window and it's after eleven in the morning. Luckily, it's one of those Professional Days when teachers work and we don't have school. I cross the hall to say hi to Jake, only he's not in his room. A panicky feeling starts in my stomach.

Then I hear Mom's voice down the hall, singing "John Jacob Jingleheimer Schmidt." And I know everything—every*one*—is fine. It's one of her "happy" songs. When she sings a sad song, like "Yesterday" or "Fix You," it's time to worry.

I find Mom on the sofa with Jake, who's looking cozy and content with a bottle of milk.

"Hey, Jake. Looks like you're feeling better!" I squeeze his little foot.

"He is." Freddy's on the rug with his freckle-faced buddy, Tyler, working on a *Star Wars* Lego set.

Freddy grins at me, then gives one of his double-winks, and I know he's thinking my "Abracadabra" really did bring Jake home.

"Ethan, get dressed and have some breakfast," Mom says. "Daniel will be here soon."

I had almost forgotten! Daniel and I are going to see the latest Marvel movie. Brian was supposed to go, too, but his parents grounded him for turning in his science report late. He gets grounded a lot.

After a quick breakfast and an even quicker shower, I'm dressed and ready to go just as Freddy runs into my room, Tyler at his side. "Can we try the trumpet trick? Jake's sleeping."

"The trumpet trick" is something I came up with a few days ago because Jake's a very unusual sleeper.

"Where's Mom?" I ask. This is an important question because, even though I know the trumpet won't wake Jake, she'll get mad, and I'll get in trouble.

"In the shower," Freddy-the-Informant tells me.

I grab my trumpet and the three of us head to Jake's room. I open the door and check to make sure he's still sleeping.

"For the first time ever," I announce, "you are about to witness the astonishing, the amazing, the unbelievable, Super Jake! He'll sleep through *anything*!"

I lift the trumpet to my lips and play the first few measures of "Jingle Bell Rock" every bit as loudly as we do in band.

Jake does not budge. Jake does not blink.

"Wow," Tyler says. "And he's not deaf or anything, right?"

"You know he's not," I answer.

"It's magic," Freddy says, his face as serious as it ever gets.

Tyler smiles. "Do it again!"

I'm a few bars into the *Harry Potter* theme song when Mom walks in wearing a fuzzy purple bathrobe, her curly wet hair dripping onto Jake's floor. "Ethan! What are you doing?"

"Uh-oh," Freddy says.

"Oh, you know. Just . . . practicing."

"Jake is trying to sleep!" Only Mom can whisper in a mad voice.

"It's okay," Tyler informs her. "It's magic."

Unfortunately, no magic trick can get me out of this.

Mom turns to Freddy. "Why don't you and Tyler get a snack?" That's Mom code for "I need to yell at Ethan in private."

I shake my head at Freddy, hoping he and Tyler will stick around so maybe Mom will get distracted and forget about being mad.

But a nanosecond later, Freddy and Tyler are outta there. So much for that idea.

"What on earth were you thinking?" Mom asks. I'm pretty sure it's one of those rhetorical questions Ms. Carlin taught us about, when you don't really expect an answer.

"Shhh," I whisper. "You'll wake Jake up."

"Right." Mom rolls her eyes. "Your trumpet blasting an inch from his ear won't wake him up, but my voice . . ."

Just then, on cue, good old Jake opens those big blue eyes of his.

"Look who's awake!" Mom coos. Her anger dissolves, and she wraps her arms around him.

If that's not magic, I don't know what is.

———————

"They really should make a movie about Loki," Daniel says.

The show ended a few minutes ago. It was epic! Now we're outside the theater, waiting for Daniel's dad to pick us up.

"You say that after every single Marvel movie." I take a sip of my leftover lemonade.

"Dude. Think about it. He's smart, funny . . ."

"Hey, I like Loki as much as you. But he doesn't care about doing the right thing. He only cares about himself. He's cool, but he's no hero."

Daniel smiles. "Not like Magnus, right?"

"Right! He's not just a great magician; he's a great person. Did I tell you that he traveled to West Africa last year and raised over fifty thousand dollars to fight hunger and poverty?" I smile at Daniel. "Can you see Loki doing that?"

He laughs. "Probably not." He finishes his soda and throws the cup in the trash can. "So, speaking of your hero, you still thinking about Magic Fest?"

"It's *all* I'm thinking about. No one wants to meet Magnus as much as I do." I swallow some more lemonade. "Remember when Jake was born and my grandparents stayed with Freddy and me because our parents were at the hospital all the time?"

"I remember," Daniel says. "It was a really tough time for you and your family."

I nod. "It was. Then one night we were sitting around switching channels on TV and there was this guy with long hair and a silver tux talking in a British accent. He'd just finished a trick and the audience was going crazy, and my grandfather turned to me and said, 'Buddy, that's the first time I've seen you smile in days.'"

It makes me smile even now, remembering it.

"So that's when you started to love magic?"

I nod. "And Magnus."

"Why do you think you loved it so much?" Daniel asks.

It's the first time anyone has asked; the first time I've really thought about it. "I don't know. Maybe seeing someone do something impossible made me think that *anything* was possible. Maybe it gave me hope or something." Now that I've said it aloud, I feel stupid. "That probably doesn't make any sense."

"No," Daniel says softly. "I get it."

"I guess maybe Bubba did, too. The next day, he bought my first magic kit."

It was the best present I ever got: shiny little silver balls and big plastic red ones; yellow sponge ducks; a deck of trick cards; a book of instructions. It even came with a little black wand. I spent that whole afternoon and evening learning my first tricks.

"The next morning," I tell Daniel, "two weeks after he was born, Jake finally came home from the hospital. And I've loved magic ever since."

He nods slowly, like everything I told him is sinking in. "You should totally go to Magic Fest."

"Thanks."

He's quiet for a moment. "But . . . how will you get there?"

I put my head in my hands. "I don't know. It's pretty expensive. Plus, I don't really have a one-person act anymore. Besides, there's no way my parents will let me go."

But what if they would? What if it turned out I could do more than entertain little kids at parties? What if, someday, I could be a great magician, too?

I should at least be able to try. When an audience laughs, or I test a new trick on someone and it works—it's the best feeling ever. I just need a way to get there. And a way to convince my parents to let me go.

Talk about magic tricks.

CHAPTER FIVE

When Daniel's dad drops me off, there's an extra car in our driveway, which means one of Jake's therapists is here. Dad says we have "a revolving door" of therapists. Every weekday one comes to our house: there are two physical therapists, two vision therapists, and one occupational therapist—her name is Mandy. It's her job to get Jake to talk and eat. The talking isn't happening yet, but the eating sure is.

My grandmother meets me at the door and squishes me into a hug. I hug her back.

"I didn't know you were coming over today, Emma."

She smiles at me. "Your brothers and I have big plans."

"Hi, sweetie," Mom calls from the kitchen, where she's watching Mandy work with Jake. "How was the movie?"

"Great," I tell her. Before I can get another word in, Freddy bursts into the room, followed by Bubba. "Ethan!" Freddy shouts. "Guess what? We're getting our Halloween costumes today! I'm gonna be Captain America! Or Spider-Man . . ." He thinks a minute. "Maybe Batman."

Bubba laughs. "Sounds like you've got a lot of great ideas, buddy."

"That's a wrap," Mandy announces as she stands up. "Good job, Jake!" She bends over and ruffles his hair, then hands him to Mom, who gives him a kiss.

Mandy packs up her stuff and heads out. Freddy's bouncing up and down, anxious to get moving.

Mom carries Jake over and stuffs him into his puffy blue teddy bear coat.

"Ethan," Freddy says, "wanna come with us?"

"That's okay, you go ahead. Be sure to find Jake a good costume, okay?"

Emma and Bubba help Freddy and Jake into their car, then wave goodbye.

Suddenly, like magic, I've got Mom all to myself. She looks at me and smiles. "Wow. I almost don't know what to do with myself."

"How long do you think they'll be gone?"

"Oh, probably a couple of hours. Why?"

Fifteen minutes later, we're at our favorite diner, just the two of us. Like old times.

"I'm so glad you thought of this, Ethan," Mom says.

"Me too." I grab packets of sugar and sweetener and start building a house. "So, what do you think Jake will be this Halloween?"

"Something terrifying, I'm sure." She smiles. "Maybe Frankenstein."

"Or a blood-sucking vampire." I laugh, picturing Jake with fangs and a huge black cape.

Mom laughs, too. "I can see it now. He'll have a—"

Before she can finish her sentence, our favorite waitress shows up with her spiky pink hair and a big smile. "Look who's here! Long time, no see. One decaf, one milk, one grilled cheese, hold the tomato, extra pickle on the side. Right?"

Mom and I nod and smile back. It's weird how nothing has changed here at the diner, when our lives are so different now.

"And for dessert?" she asks.

Mom and I answer at the same time. I say, "Hot fudge sundae," while she orders cherry pie à la mode.

After the waitress brings our drinks, Mom stirs sugar and cream into her coffee while I add more packs of sweetener to my house. I've gotten pretty good at building these houses over the years. Bubba says it takes "a certain finesse." Kind of like bringing up a certain subject at the exact right place and time.

"Mom?"

"Here ya go!" The waitress gives us each a plate with half a grilled cheese sandwich, chips, and extra pickles. "I'll bring dessert once you're done."

Mom thanks her. I would, too, but my mouth's already full.

We spend the next few minutes enjoying the food and the time away from . . . everything. Before I know it, we're on to dessert.

For a minute, the gooey hot fudge and my favorite coconut ice cream distract me from my mission. Then Mom dips her spoon into my dessert and pushes her pie toward me. I take a bite of sweet cherry and make a mental note to order it again whenever we come back. I hope it will be soon. It's nice having Mom to myself for a change.

We're going to run out of time if I don't say something soon. I take a deep breath. "Remember when Brian visited his grandparents last summer?" I lean forward. "He flew three thousand miles by himself, all the way to California."

Mom drains her coffee cup. "I know. His mom was terrified something would go wrong. I don't blame her."

This is not what I want to hear. "He was fine."

"Still. I can't imagine him flying all that way alone."

"He wasn't alone. There were other passengers and flight attendants and probably somebody flying the plane," I joke.

Mom doesn't even crack a smile. "Well, there's no way I'd let *you* do that!" She stabs a piece of pie with her fork.

This is not going well. "What if I wasn't alone and it was less than two hundred miles away?"

Mom puts down her fork and looks me in the eyes. "Ethan, what is this about?"

"It's about a once-in-a-lifetime chance." I tell her the rest as fast as I can, barely stopping to take a breath. Trying to get it all out before she says—

"I'm sorry, sweetie. I really can't see that happening."

I groan. "It's much closer than California, plus you or Dad would be with me. And we don't even have to fly, we can—"

"Enough." She puts her hand on my arm. "No one is going to Atlantic City."

"Why not?"

"We have way too much going on."

"You mean, Jake?" I pull my arm away, accidentally hitting the sugar packet house. It collapses, along with my plans.

Mom puts her hand in her lap. "I'm sorry."

There's got to be some way to change her mind. I eat my sundae as slowly as possible while I rack my brain for a way to convince her. I've got maybe two teaspoonfuls left when her cell phone rings. She grabs it on the second ring. Worry spreads across her face.

I hold my breath.

"Hello?" She listens, then exhales. "That's fine, Dad. Thanks. Have fun!" She ends the call and smiles. "Costumes are a success. They're moving on to frozen yogurt."

I smile back, then get a sudden flash of inspiration. "Maybe Bubba can go with me!"

"To New Jersey?"

I nod so fast I probably look like a bobblehead.

"I don't know," Mom says in slow motion. "It's asking an awful lot."

Like no one ever asks me *to do anything?* I don't say it out loud, though. I never do. What's the point? I stare at the puddle of ice cream in the bowl.

Mom sighs. "Your dad and I will talk about it, okay? Just don't get your hopes up."

I jump out of my seat and give her a bone-crushing hug.

CHAPTER SIX

Today's party is *Star Wars*–themed. I'm surrounded by miniature Han Solos, Luke Skywalkers, and Reys. Wendy, the birthday girl, is turning four. She is dressed in Princess Leia's white gown, and has those weird buns on either side of her head (except her hair is red). I already know her favorite color is purple and her favorite candy is anything chocolate, so I've got plenty of both ready for my magic act.

The group of kids settles on the rug in front of me while Wendy's mom dims the lights and Freddy starts the music. As the opening notes of the *Star Wars* theme song play, the audience falls silent.

It's showtime.

Freddy's candy vanishes on cue; SpongeBob makes a surprise appearance; and I pull forty-six feet of purple paper out of my mouth. Parents applaud, kids laugh or gasp in amazement. Everything goes perfectly.

I'm waving my wand over the top hat to make chocolate candy appear when Wendy's mom says, "Sweetheart! You almost missed the entire show!"

I look up to see a red-headed giant in the doorway—Ned. The sight of him towering over a dozen little kids is as funny as it is unexpected. Wendy runs over and gives him a hug. "You're here!" she shouts.

Ned bends down and hugs her back, and suddenly I see the resemblance.

"Ethan," their mom says, "this is my son—"

"Ned." I nod.

"Hey," he says. Which is almost more than he's said to me at school. Maybe it's time for that to change. And maybe it's up to me to change it. "Wendy, want your big brother to be in the show?" I ask.

She smiles and claps her hands.

Freddy looks confused, and I don't blame him; I'm improvising a little. I hand Freddy a stack of "Miller's Magic" flyers and wink. He winks back by blinking both eyes.

Ned doesn't wink. Or smile. I'm starting to think this is a bad idea, but his mom gives him a gentle push in my direction. "It'll be fun," she says.

I hope she's right. I tell him, "C'mon up!" Then I grab a

deck of cards and shuffle.

He trudges over like I'm about to pull out one of his teeth. I smile and say, "Pick a card, any card."

He rolls his eyes, but takes one.

"Okay, show the audience, then put it back in the deck."

I notice my so-called assistant making paper airplanes out of my "Miller's Magic" flyers. "Freddy! What're you doing?" I give him a dirty look. "Excuse me," I tell Ned. I go over to Freddy, grab my flyers, walk back, and shuffle again.

"All right." I pull out the ace of clubs. "Is this your card?"

He shakes his head.

"Okay, hold on. Is this it?" I show him the five of hearts.

He folds his arms across his chest and under his breath says, "I can't believe my mom is paying you for this."

I keep my smile on for the audience, but it's not easy.

"I've seen better acts on *Sesame Street*," he says . . . and not quietly, either.

It's getting harder to smile. Then I hear Freddy say, "You watch *Sesame Street*?"

Ned opens his mouth, but nothing comes out.

Now, it's easy to smile . . . and hard not to laugh.

I wave the card in front of Ned's face. "Are you sure this isn't your card?" I ask again.

"I already told you no," Ned says, his face turning pink.

"Is this it?" my assistant asks.

Everyone turns to see Freddy holding the queen of diamonds.

Ned's eyes bug out. "Wait? How did . . . ?"

"Oh, you know." I shrug. "I saw it on *Sesame Street.*"

Now Ned's face is almost as red as his hair. He looks like he wants to hurt me. "Thanks," he says. "This was super fun." Only by the *way* he says it, and the way he *looks* when he says it, I'm pretty sure he doesn't mean it.

"Hey," I tell him, "I wasn't trying to—"

"Whatever." He turns his back to me and walks out of the room. Something tells me the next time Ned sees me probably won't be "super fun," either. Luckily, it's three days from now, since there's no school on Monday. Maybe he'll have forgotten about it by then. I'm sure not gonna bring it up.

I take a deep breath, exhale, and finish the show. As usual, everything goes smoothly, and I've just finished packing up my supplies when the doorbell rings.

Wendy's mom opens the door. It's Mom, but she's alone. The crazy thing is, instead of feeling relieved, I'm worried. Why isn't Jake with her? Still, she doesn't look like anything's wrong. In fact, she looks really happy.

"Rox?" She stares at Wendy's mom.

"Bex!" Wendy's mom shouts.

Bex?

They squeal like teenage girls and throw their arms around each other, and I wonder if I've landed in an alternate universe.

They let go but keep grinning and staring, like this is the best thing that ever happened to either of them. "What are you doing here?" Mom asks.

"We moved over the summer." Wendy's mom leans over and lowers her voice, but I can still hear her. "Bob and I split up last year."

Before either of them can say another word, or explain to me what the heck is going on, Freddy comes running. "Mommy! I want a *Star Wars* party, too! I want a red lightsaber like Darth Vader. Or a blue one, like Luke. Or—"

"These are your boys?" Wendy's mom asks mine.

"They sure are." Mom wraps one arm around me and the other around Freddy.

Wendy's mom smiles. "I can totally see their dad . . ."

"Where?" Freddy turns and looks behind us.

Mom laughs. "She means, you guys look like your dad—handsome."

Freddy's big eyes get even bigger. "You know Daddy?"

"I do," Wendy's mom says. "We went to the same college."

"You haven't aged one day," Mom says to her, then turns

♦ 44 ♦

back to Freddy and me. "We lived on the same floor in the dorm for four years. Can you believe it?"

Nope. I can't. It's bad enough that Wendy's mom—Rox—is related to Ned. Now she and Mom are friends?

Before things get any stranger, Wendy runs in saying something about Duck, Duck, Goose and her mom and mine promise to get together soon.

Talk about super fun . . .

CHAPTER SEVEN

The good news is, I'm not going to school today, even though it's Monday. The bad news is, I'm going to synagogue instead.

Dad peeks into my room. "Five minutes."

"Ready."

Dad straightens my tie and gives it a pat. "Looking sharp, E." He winks at me.

"How do *I* look?" Freddy asks, interrupting as always. His clip-on tie is lopsided, his shirt is half out of his pants, and he's got grape jelly smeared on his cheek.

I squeeze my foot into a dress shoe. "You look like a—"

Dad clears his throat. "Not today, Ethan." He bends down and tries to make Freddy presentable. "You look very grown-up," he tells him.

The reason we're wearing suits, and that I can't make fun of Freddy, is that it's Yom Kippur—the holiest day of the year, if you're Jewish. On Yom Kippur, you fast for twenty-four hours if you're thirteen or older. Last year, I lasted eighteen. This year I'm shooting for twenty. I figure if I fast two more hours each year, I'll be right on schedule. (Take that, Miss Wright!)

Another thing about Yom Kippur is that you pray God will forgive you for what you did wrong, and are sorry for, over the past year, and that you'll be written in the Book of Life for another year to come. I know there's not an actual book. I mean, how big would that have to be? Still, pretty much every practicing Jew on the planet prays today.

The parking lot is totally full when we arrive at the synagogue, except for the handicapped spaces. We pull into one of those.

"We're lucky we can park here, huh?" Freddy says.

No one answers.

My brothers and I wait in the crowded lobby while Mom says hi to someone I don't know and Dad puts on his prayer shawl. After what feels like forever, Freddy walks down the hall to the little kid service, while I head into the sanctuary with my parents and Jake. As usual, because of the Kid Kart, we sit at the end of a row.

Mom hands me a prayer book, and I try to follow along. When everyone reads out loud in English, I do, too. When we pray in Hebrew, I join in as much as I can. When the choir sings, I chime in, and when the rabbi starts his sermon, I try to pay attention. Once in a while, though, my mind drifts off.

I imagine my first meeting with Magnus the Magnificent. Maybe he'll smile and we'll shake hands. Maybe we'll be super cool and not even have to say anything, just nod at each other. Or maybe I'll be so excited, I won't be *able* to say anything. . . .

"Ethan." Mom nudges me. She's got this crazy radar thing and can always tell when I'm not paying attention. It's really annoying.

"Today we reflect on our past and pray for our future, and the futures of our loved ones," the rabbi says. "We pray for good health and happiness. For peace and safety. We pray for our husbands and wives, mothers and fathers, sons and daughters." He nods to the ushers on either side of the sanctuary and they head down the aisles, passing out papers.

Once we all have one, the rabbi says, "Please take a copy of this home, and take it to heart."

It's called "A Prayer for Children," by Ina Hughs. And it's actually more like a poem than a prayer. It talks about kids who "sneak popsicles" and kids who "never get dessert." Kids who "get visits from the tooth fairy" and kids "who have never seen a dentist."

Ms. Carlin would like it a lot, and I'm thinking about showing it to her tomorrow. Then we get to the last stanza: "We pray for children / who want to be carried / and for those who must, / for those we never give up on / and for those who don't get a second chance. . . ."

I hear Mom taking short, fast breaths beside me. I look over and, sure enough, she's crying.

"Ethan," Dad whispers, leaning over Mom. "Get Freddy. We'll meet you in the lobby."

I nod and head to Freddy's classroom, glad to get out of there. He sees me right away and jumps up. "Are we leaving already?" he asks with a big smile.

At least somebody's happy.

———————

We get back from synagogue tired and hungry. Mom gives Jake a bottle and some oatmeal/banana mush while Dad fixes Freddy a roast beef sandwich.

"How about you, E?" Dad smears mustard onto the bread. "You don't have to fast for two more years, y'know."

"That's all right. I'm gonna go four more hours."

"Okay," he says. "If you're sure."

"Yep. No big deal." My stomach growls so loudly they'd hear it on Mars. The roast beef smells amazing. I'm hungry enough to eat the mustard by itself.

"Mom and I are going to take a nap," Dad says. "Maybe you should, too. It makes the fast go faster—haha."

I think about it for a minute or two, but I'm too hungry to sleep, so I visit Jake. He's in bed, eyes wide open, waiting for me.

"Hey, Jake!" I sit down and scoop him into my lap so we're facing each other. "Did you have a yummy lunch? I'm so hungry, even baby food sounds good! But I'm not complaining. Maybe if I fast when I don't have to, God might give me some bonus points. They sure could come in handy—for both of us." I bounce him up and down on my knees, then stop before his food makes a second appearance.

"Want me to blow some bubbles for you or read *Peter Rabbit*?" Even though he won't answer, I still like to give him choices. "How 'bout we play school?" I Velcro him into his little chair and slide the plastic tray on top: his very own desk. It's weird how fun school is when it's pretend. Plus, I'm a much nicer teacher than Miss Wright is.

I squeeze Jake's hands and pull them back and forth as fast as I can. He gives me a super-huge grin to let me know he's ready. "Let's start with English. Do you know what a synonym is?" He gazes at me, waiting for the answer. "It's two different words that mean the same thing. Like I could say, 'Freddy is dumb,' or 'Freddy is stupid.'" Except either way I'd get in trouble.

"Then there are homonyms. They sound the same but

mean different things. Like *two*, *too*, and *to*." I squeeze his hands again, then raise two of his fingers. "See? *Two* fingers. Then there's, 'I want *to* eat.'" My stomach growls. "I think I'm *too* hungry to teach." I picture Freddy's roast beef sandwich. My mouth is watering and my stomach is rumbling even louder than before. Would it really matter if I have a little snack?

Will it matter if I don't?

I go to Jake's bookcase, grab a red wand that lights up, and place it on his tray. I turn it on, wrap his fingers around it, and help him wave it back and forth. Then I push it toward him, just a little, hoping he'll reach out for it, or at least try to.

He hasn't yet, but maybe this time he will. I am fasting, after all. I wave it around some more. His eyes watch, but his hands are still. Like always.

I think of the "Prayer for Children." Will Jake always have to be carried? I close my eyes and ask God not just to put Jake in the Book of Life, but to give him a better life.

I open my eyes and see him looking back at me. I take his hand and, together, we reach for the red wand.

CHAPTER EIGHT

I'm dreading school today because I have to see Ned for the first time since Wendy's birthday party. Plus, in case once isn't enough, I have to see him twice: in both gym and English.

I'm not that worried about English class; I know Ms. Carlin will protect me. (I hope.)

But gym class? Things could get ugly.

We just started our basketball unit, which is good news for me. I'm not all that athletic, but I'm a fast runner and—not to brag or anything—I'm especially good at foul shots.

Basketball aside, I'm not looking forward to being anywhere near Ned. My strategy is to act like nothing happened. I'm hoping he'll do the same. I'm hoping we can move on or, at least, keep out of each other's way.

"Split off into pairs and let's do some drills," Mr. Davis, our gym teacher, says. Then he calls out our names and pairs us up.

One guess who I get.

Whenever Mr. Davis turns his back, instead of throwing the ball *to* me, Ned throws it *at* me. One time the ball hits my arm really hard, and I know I'll have a big purple bruise there tomorrow. But I don't let Ned see how much it hurts. Instead, I smile and hurl the ball back as hard as I can.

Fun times.

Almost as fun as math is during sixth period.

"Ethan, what did you get for question eight?" Miss Wright glares in my direction.

"Uh . . . nothing?"

"The value of x is nothing?"

Hey, maybe it is! "Yep. X is nothing. Zero."

Some classmates smile, knowing I took a wild shot like always.

My teacher sighs that special way she saves just for me. "Would anyone *else* care to hazard a guess?"

———————————

After three billion years, it's finally time for seventh period.

I'd do just about anything to sit with Brian again, but it seems Ned and I are both happy to ignore each other. It's pretty easy to pretend he's not there, since he never says anything anyway. I do my best to pay attention to Ms. Carlin.

She's talking about our next unit, which is all about heroes.

I smile to myself, remembering my ongoing Loki debate with Daniel.

First off, Ms. Carlin asks us to make a collective list of what it means to be a hero. Some things we come up with are: someone who stands out from the crowd and will be remembered long after he (or she) dies; someone who does something amazing; or someone who is in an impossible situation but keeps trying and never gives up.

"Here are some definitions from Webster's dictionary." Ms. Carlin holds it up and reads from the page: "Someone 'admired for his'"—she smiles and adds—"'or *her* achievements and noble qualities,' 'one that shows great courage,' and 'the central figure in an event.'"

She looks around the room. "I want you all to think about who your hero is and why. Each of you will prepare both a written and oral presentation worth forty percent of your final grade."

While groans explode all around me, I'm totally psyched because I've already got my hero picked out: Magnus the Magnificent! I know so much about him; I could almost give the report today. A little bit of work and, abracadabra: A+!

After class, I tell Ms. Carlin about Magic Fest.

"The winner gets to meet Magnus?" she asks.

"And perform with him!"

"Meet him? In person?"

"Um, yeah."

Ms. Carlin sits down at her desk, then grabs her big red Maryland Terrapins water cup and drains it. "Where is this competition?"

"New Jersey," I answer, wondering why she's acting so weird.

"And what is the date?"

"Well, the competition is January nineteenth through the twenty-first, but—"

"January nineteenth . . ." She pulls a mini calendar out of a drawer, and I see a picture of a guy with long hair wearing a silver tux.

"Is that a Magnus the Magnificent calendar?" I ask.

Ms. Carlin's face turns pink. "Why, yes. Yes, it is." She clears her throat. "Now, this competition . . . I assume it's open to the public?"

"I guess?"

She pushes a piece of hair away from her face, then leans forward in her seat. "So, just to be clear. You're saying Magnus will be in New Jersey on January nineteenth—"

"Oh. No. He won't actually be at the competition."

She blinks. "He won't?"

"Nope. The winner meets him some other time and place 'to be determined.'"

"Oh." Her shoulders relax and she leans back in her seat, then reaches for her cup before realizing it's empty.

"The problem is convincing my dad to let me go. I'm sort of waiting for the right time to ask him." Like when I get straight A's *and* win the Nobel Peace Prize.

"I see," Ms. Carlin says. "Will this help?" She reaches into a folder, riffles through some papers, and hands me the test on Acts I through III of *A Midsummer Night's Dream*. I got forty-eight out of fifty questions right.

"It might!"

On the way home I plan my strategy. First, timing is important. I only have Mom's attention ten minutes tops before I get Freddy at the bus stop. I try to imagine her questions and my answers:

Question: Even if we say yes, who's going to pay for all this?
Answer: I will!

Q: How?
A: With money.

Q: What money?
A: That's a good question.

My favorite way to make money, of course, is doing magic shows. And, as luck would have it, I've just lined up another.

This one is for Katie, a member of "the Group."

"The Group" is Katie, Peter, C.K., and Jake, plus their moms. They get together when they can, which isn't very often, since the kids get sick a lot. Today they're meeting at a fast-food place, and I'm tagging along so Katie's mom can go over details for the party.

Katie is around Freddy's age and has hearing aids, purple-framed glasses, blond braids, and Down syndrome. And she's a hugger. Whether she knows you or not.

Peter is about a year older than I am and has cerebral palsy. He's in a wheelchair and has a hard time walking and talking. The first time we met, he had a seizure. Sometimes he tries to feed himself and spills his food all over the place. (I do that sometimes, too.) He "talks" by using this board with letters and numbers. He's really smart and really funny. He's definitely my favorite person in "the Group" (except for Jake, of course).

Then there's C.K. (short for Constantine Koroulakis). He's nine years old and has autism. Unlike Katie who talks nonstop, and Peter who talks in his own way, C.K. never talks at all. He hates loud noises and stares at shiny things and avoids eye contact with the rest of us. If he's super hungry or overtired, though, watch out! He can have some serious temper tantrums.

So, when it comes to the Group, things always get a little . . . complicated. Still, magic is magic and money is money and I'll do just about anything to get to Magic Fest.

"Originally I was planning to invite only girls," Katie's mom shouts over the loud laughter and conversation around us. "But you know Katie. She's awfully fond of boys."

She sure is, I think to myself. That very second, she's wrapping her arms around some random teenage guy who looks terrified. "Uh, is it okay if Katie's, uh . . ." I nod my head in her direction.

"Oh, for goodness' sake." She stands up and waves her arms to get her daughter's attention. "Katie!"

"Sit," my mom says. "I'll get her." Mom goes off to save the day, knowing Jake will wait patiently in his Kid Kart for her to come back.

Katie's mom sighs. "I keep telling her she can't go around hugging everyone she sees."

I'm not sure how to respond, so I shrug.

"Anyway . . . what was I saying?" she asks.

Beats me. It's impossible to think when the Group is around. C.K. is hitting himself in the forehead while his mom tries to distract him with a French fry and Peter knocks over his drink. Even though the cup has a lid and a straw, half the soda spills onto the floor.

"Ethan?" Peter's mom asks. "I'm sorry. Would you mind...?"

"No problem." I get up and head for the counter to grab a pile of napkins for the third time in ten minutes.

"Ethan!" Katie smiles like she hasn't seen me in months. She throws her arms around me and squeezes. Hard.

I sort of hug her back, then grab some napkins before we head back to our peaceful little table together.

Peter has moved on to dessert and gotten more of his sundae on the table than in his stomach. Before Katie's mom and I can get back to our conversation, C.K. launches himself onto the floor and starts kicking and screaming his head off. His mom and mine kneel down beside him while Katie hugs Peter and knocks the ice cream off his spoon.

"Ethan?" Katie's mom shouts to be heard, even though I'm two inches away. "Y'know what? I'm thinking maybe this would be simpler over the phone."

A few minutes after we get home, Katie's mom calls, and soon we've got everything worked out. I add Katie's birthday party to the calendar on my phone. As I scroll down to January, I see the date for Magic Fest and a chill goes through my spine.

I still haven't had a chance to talk to Dad. Between Freddy making a mess and Mom taking care of Jake, mealtimes are too chaotic. After dinner, my parents take turns putting my brothers to bed. By the time Jake's had his bath and Freddy's gotten as many bedtime stories as he can, Mom and Dad just want to watch TV or go to sleep themselves.

I scroll back up to the October calendar. It's almost Halloween. It's no surprise that this is Freddy's favorite day of the year (all the sugar he can eat!); the funny thing is, it's Dad's, too. Which means he'll be in an especially great mood this weekend.

Which means it will be the perfect time to bring up Magic Fest.

CHAPTER NINE

Mandy's green station wagon is in our driveway when I get home from school, which means I won't be snacking alone. Every week she lets Jake try something different: a new cup or spoon or, best of all, a new food.

I drop my trumpet and backpack on the floor, then go to the kitchen where Mandy and Jake are hanging out.

"Hey, Jake!"

He tries to smile back, but it's tough with Mandy's fingers in his mouth.

"What's Jakey gonna try today?" Freddy calls out as he and Mom come in from the carport. "Another lollipop?" he asks, his eyes full of hope. Last week, Jake got to lick a cherry lollipop and Mandy gave Freddy one, too.

Mandy smiles. "Not today." She whispers the mystery ingredient to me, and I head for the fridge to get it, along with chocolate milk for Freddy and me.

Jake's the adventurous type, especially when it comes to food. The thing is, a lot of stuff is off-limits since he doesn't know how to chew yet. Still, you'd be surprised how many things Mandy comes up with.

I bring today's experiment to the table and she squirts a dab of whipped cream onto her finger and offers it to Jake. As usual, he makes a funny face at the taste and feel of something new, then sticks out his tongue for more.

"All right, Jake!" Mandy laughs.

Mom smiles. "He likes it."

I grab a spoon. "Can I give him some?"

"Can I have some?" That's Freddy for you.

A few minutes later, Mandy says goodbye, and Mom goes downstairs to catch up on e-mail while Jake takes a nap in his Kid Kart. Since the whipped cream is already on the table, I decide to make good use of it by making banana splits for Freddy and me. We're a few bites in, and talking about my favorite thing (hint: rhymes with *tragic*), when he says, "I almost forgot!"

He jumps out of his seat, runs into the living room, and rummages around in his Captain America backpack. A minute later, he hands me a crumpled-up, banana split–sticky piece of paper.

"What's this?"

"Names for your magic act!" He bounces up and down, waiting for my response.

I unfold the paper and try to read his handwriting:

Ethan the Great

Ethan the Greatest

Ethan the Encredible
(Spelling's not his best subject.)

The Ethan & Freddy Show

"What do you think?"

"I think you've got butterscotch all over your face."

He wipes half of it off. "I like the last one best, don't you?"

"Uh . . ." I go with what Mom says when Dad gives her a present she doesn't like: "It's . . . interesting."

"Which do you like best?"

So much for Mom's technique. I try Dad's: changing the subject. "More ice cream?"

Freddy looks at his still-full bowl and shakes his head.

Have I mentioned Freddy's the World's Slowest Eater?

He's also determined to make me choose from his list. I don't want to hurt his feelings, but I'm running out of things to say. Luckily, Jake comes to the rescue, as usual, by opening his big blue eyes.

"Jake! You're awake." I unbuckle him, lift him out of his Kid Kart, and settle him on my lap. "Ladies and gentlemen." I hold an invisible microphone close to my mouth. "Boys and girls. It's time for another exciting episode of—"

"Food Island!" Freddy shouts through a mouthful of mint chip.

In case you've never heard of Food Island, it's the thrilling tale of a heroic knight, Sir Jake, and his noble steed, Potato Latke. Sir Jake is on a quest to rescue the fair Tina (his babysitter) from the evil, fire-breathing Toothy Ruthie. Trouble is, there's so much yummy stuff on Food Island that he always gets a little sidetracked.

"Ethan? D'you think that'll really happen?" Freddy asks after the stunning conclusion, where Jake sweeps Tina off her feet and into his arms, and they eat pizza and fries to their hearts' content.

"Probably not. There aren't many fire-breathing dragons here in Maryland."

"No," he says, no trace of a smile on his anxious face. "Will Jake ever eat pizza?"

"I dunno, Freddy. Will you ever finish your banana split?" Instead of laughing, he just looks at me, waiting for an answer I don't have.

I grab his bowl of ice cream soup and pour the melted mess into the sink. "Wanna play video games?"

He zips out of the room.

I heft Jake into his Kid Kart and wheel him over to keep us company. Before I know it, my hand is on the controller.

But my mind is still on Freddy's question.

Since Halloween is almost here, as soon as dinner's over and homework is done, we get to work. Like I said, it's Dad's favorite holiday. He makes a whole production out of it: spooky decorations; scary music; scarier stories; horror movies. But the first thing every year is our jack-o'-lantern.

Dad sits in the middle of the living room with a gigantic pumpkin on a pile of newspaper. Freddy and I are next to him, cross-legged on the carpet, while Mom and Jake watch from the sofa.

"Okay," Dad says as he expertly slices the top off the pumpkin. "What will it be this year? Funny? Silly? Beautiful?" He winks at Mom. "Or scary?" He wiggles his eyebrows at Freddy.

"Scary!" Freddy shouts.

Dad grabs a sheet of paper and starts drawing ideas for

the face, while Freddy and I share the best job of all: scooping out slimy goo and pumpkin seeds with our fingers. Usually, I "accidentally" get some in his dirty blond hair, making it dirty orange. Then Mom gets mad at me and has to help him wash it out. Even though it's one of my favorite things about Halloween, this time I resist. I can't risk making her angry until Magic Fest is over.

It's gonna be a *long* ten weeks.

After Freddy and I separate seeds from goo, Mom sprinkles the seeds with cinnamon sugar and roasts them in the oven. While Dad carves the pumpkin, Mom makes a batch of cookie dough. I cut out witches and cats, and Freddy dyes the icing (and his hands) orange and black. The cookies are another reason I love Halloween. Dad's a great cook, but Mom loves to bake. At least, she used to; now she doesn't have time—unless it's a special occasion, like Halloween.

While the cookies bake, we try on our costumes. Like always, Freddy-the-Predictable dresses as Darth Vader. I, of course, am a magician in a black cape and top hat. Poor old Jake is stuck with a Winnie the Pooh outfit Emma claimed was "adorable." It's not a very dignified look, but Jake doesn't complain.

When it comes to Halloween, I don't complain much either. After all, getting a ton of candy just for wearing a costume is a pretty "sweet" deal. The only thing I don't like is that Houdini died on Halloween night back in 1926. That makes tonight bittersweet, instead of sweet.

After Mom oohs and aahs over our costumes, we change into pj's and snack on pumpkin seeds, apple cider, and cookies. Dad lights a candle inside the pumpkin and I turn off the lamps. With the spooky face glowing in the darkness, the whole house smelling like cinnamon and cloves, and Jake warm and cozy in my lap, I wish every day were Halloween.

CHAPTER TEN

It's surprising enough when someone is knocking on my door in the middle of the night. (Okay, actually it's 7:00 a.m., but on Saturday morning it feels like the same thing.) But the real surprise is *who's* knocking: not my parents; not Freddy, since he never knocks; and, no, it's not Jake. It's Tina, Jake's babysitter.

"Wake up, sleepyhead!"

"What are you doing here?" I ask, more asleep than awake.

She wiggles her eyebrows and says, "Hurry up and get dressed if you want to find out." She smiles then closes my bedroom door. I hear her retreating down the hallway.

Sleepy but curious, I throw on jeans and a T-shirt and yawn my way into the living room. Mom is sitting cross-legged on the floor, sorting through Jake's big Winnie the Pooh bag. Dad's in the rocking chair, drinking his morning coffee, typing something into his GPS. I go over to take a peek, but he gives a sly smile and turns it over so I can't see.

Tina and Jake are on the sofa, busy with one of his all-time favorite activities: breakfast. I sit next to them and rub Jake's foot. "Hey, Jake, do you know what the surprise is?"

Tina grins. "If he does, he's not saying."

"Tina!" Freddy rushes in and throws himself at her and Jake.

"Careful!" Mom cries. "Jake's trying to drink."

Tina winks at Freddy, who does his usual double-blink back.

Dad heads toward the kitchen, saying, "Mom wants you to eat before we go."

"Go where?"

He and Mom share one of their conspiratorial smiles.

"I can't even think of food this early," I moan.

"Yeah, I'm not even awake," Freddy chimes in.

Dad comes back with one hand behind his back. "That's a shame. Guess I'll have to enjoy these all by my lonesome." He shows us a bag of doughnuts.

"Maybe I could eat *something* . . ." I reach for one with strawberry icing and sprinkles.

After a delicious helping of a doughnut or two, the six of us pile into the minivan. During the drive, Jake sleeps; Dad gets lost; Tina tells funny stories about high school; Mom asks Dad to stop and get directions while Dad says he's not lost; and Freddy sleeps, wakes up, asks, "Are we there yet?" and falls asleep again.

Three hours (and two bathroom breaks) later, we pull into the massive parking lot of Kings Dominion, a gigantic amusement park Freddy and I love, but haven't been to in forever. Since it's Halloween weekend, all the workers, and lots of the visitors, are in costume, and there are huge jack-o'-lanterns and creepy spiderwebs all over the park.

"We'll meet the three of you for lunch at one o'clock by the log ride," Mom says.

"Have fun!" Dad says.

"And listen to Tina," Mom tells Freddy and me.

Before either of them can say another word, Freddy grabs Tina's hand and sprints off in a random direction. And I'm right behind.

The first thing we do is the most fun funhouse ever. Inside, a zombie comes out of nowhere and chases Tina around. She screams and laughs and screams some more. Next we do battle on the bumper cars and Freddy crashes into me again and again (mainly when he tries not to—he isn't the best driver).

After that, we explore Freddy's favorite part of the park, Planet Snoopy, which has tons of rides named after Peanuts characters, like Woodstock Whirlybirds, Sally's Sea Plane, and Lucy's Crabbie Cabbies (in case he didn't have enough bumper cars yet).

By the time we meet up for lunch, I'm seriously starving. While Dad waits in line for food and Mom gives Jake apple juice and ground-up turkey, I pull five different packets of sugar from the plastic box on our table.

"Hey, Tina, which of these do you like best?" I ask.

"The yellow," she says.

"Okay." I put the other four back. "Mom, do you have a quarter?" (Ethan's Rule #1: A good magician never uses his own money.) While Mom searches her pocketbook, I pull a small red magic marker out of my pocket. (Ethan's Rule #2: A good magician always comes prepared.)

"Here you go." Mom hands me a coin.

I thank her, then focus on Tina again. "Want to see if I can make this sweetener even sweeter?"

With a smile, Tina leans in to watch the action up close. "Go for it."

I hand her the marker and the quarter. "Mark the coin however you like," I tell her.

She draws a smiley face on it. Freddy laughs.

"Can I draw on some money, too?" he asks.

"No," Mom answers.

I sweep the coin and sweetener into my right hand. "Okay," I tell Tina, "squeeze my hand as tight as you can."

She does. She's stronger than I thought.

"You can let go now," I squeak. I shake the sugar packet, put it in my left hand, tear it with my right, and pour it onto the table . . . along with a smiley-faced quarter.

"No way!" Tina shouts.

"Cool!" Freddy giggles.

"Wow!" Mom says. "How in the world . . . ?"

I shrug. (Ethan's Rule #3: A good magician never reveals his secrets.)

After lunch, Tina hangs out with Jake while our parents take Freddy and me to the arcade. We have a blast playing Dad's favorite old game—Frogger—and Mom's favorite—Skee-Ball. Then it's finally time for *my* favorite: the log ride! For the first time, Fearless Freddy is tall enough to go on. He insists on sitting in front, and gets drenched on the final descent down the slide.

Before you can say "pneumonia," Mom hauls him off to the nearest restroom while Dad and I join Tina and Jake at a park bench nearby.

"I can't believe she brought extra clothes to an amusement park," I tell Tina.

"I can," she says with a smile. "We are talking about Freddy, after all. He was either gonna get soaked or spill something all over himself."

"Or both," we say at the same time.

As Dad tucks the blue bunny blanket around Jake, a kid around Freddy's age walks by licking a triple-decker ice-cream cone.

"Whoa!" Tina cries. "Did you see that?"

We only ate an hour ago, but something about an amusement park really gets your appetite going.

"Mom won't like it," Dad says, reading my mind. "She'll say it will ruin dinner."

"I know." I groan a little.

"So how 'bout we get two scoops instead of three?" Dad offers.

Tina stays in the shade with Jake while Dad and I walk around in search of ice cream. As we make our way through the park, it hits me: the two of us, alone together. It's the perfect opportunity to talk about Magic Fest!

Maybe too perfect. What if he says no and the whole day is ruined?

But what if he says yes?

We walk by Frankenstein twisting a purple balloon into a pig for a little girl. It's such a strange sight we both laugh. Then I take a deep breath and cross my fingers behind my back.

"Hey, Dad? I was wondering. Did Mom happen to mention—"

"A 'once-in-a-lifetime chance' to meet your hero?" He smiles.

Before I can answer, Dad says, "There's the ice cream stand," and he walks toward it.

I don't even want ice cream anymore. I'd give up a thousand cones to go to Magic Fest.

"It's asking a lot," Dad says, sounding like Mom's clone.

He's gonna say no. I knew I shouldn't have . . .

"So, you'll have to earn it," Dad says.

I freeze. Did he say what I think he said? And, more importantly, did he not say no?

He turns to face me. Hundreds of people walk by, and there's tons of noise everywhere, but all I see is his face. All I hear is his voice. It's like everything has stopped.

"First of all, your math grade has to improve. Anything below a C, the trip is off. Understood?"

I manage to nod.

"Second. When Mom asks you to help with your brothers, you do it. Right away."

That one's easy. I already do that . . . well, most of the time.

"Third. It's your responsibility to figure out how much money you and I need for food, hotel room, and the convention fee—and *you* pay two-thirds of it."

"Wait, you're going with me?"

"If that's all right with you." Dad smiles.

I smile back.

"So," he asks, "do we have a deal?" He extends his hand to me.

We shake on it, then I hug him. "Thanks, Dad." All around us, the amusement park comes back to life. We dive into the crowd and head for the ice cream stand, and I can't stop smiling. It's the best day I've ever had.

Since Jake got lots of naps in earlier, he's totally awake by the time it's dark outside. His blue eyes are wide open, like he can't get enough of the bright lights and colors of the park, or the zillions of people running around.

As soon as the sun has set, all six of us go ride the Ferris wheel. Next, we ride the carousel. The first time we ride, Jake sits between Mom and Dad on a fancy bench that doesn't move. The second time we put him on a big green horse and he rides with me. Holding him tight, I pretend we're cowboys in the Wild West, and Freddy (who's on the horse ahead of us) is the bank robber we're chasing. We never do catch him.

Jake doesn't fall asleep for one second—his eyes are wide open the whole time. I know he's having just as much fun as the rest of us.

Before we head home, we give Jake his first taste of cotton candy. Mom lets me pull a little piece off and feed it to him. His nose crinkles, his blue eyes get even wider . . . and his tongue immediately sticks out for more pink fluff.

It's the perfect night.

CHAPTER ELEVEN

"I can't believe you're going!" Daniel slathers the last of his fries with ketchup and shakes his head. "Man, you are so lucky."

"I know!" Unlike Daniel, who has already demolished his entire meal, I've been too busy talking to eat. "I'm so psyched I almost forgot to turn in my social studies paper."

Brian chokes on his root beer. "I thought it was due next week."

I shrug. "Sorry."

That pretty much ends Brian's part of the conversation, along with his appetite.

"Bummer," Daniel says, eyeing Brian's plate. "You gonna eat that burger?"

Brian shakes his head and hands it over. As Daniel bites into it, I see him checking out my bag of chips. I slide it toward him.

"The problem is, I've got to come up with almost three hundred and fifty bucks for the expenses."

"How much do you have saved up?" Daniel asks.

"Only about seventy-five dollars." I push the rest of my food in his direction. "Even if I booked a magic act every weekend between now and January nineteenth, I'd still be . . ." Eight weekends times fifteen dollars, plus my current seventy-five . . . where's a calculator when you need it?

"Around a hundred and fifty dollars short." As always, Daniel saves me from total math humiliation. Once he's finished our lunches, he buys Brian and me each an ice cream sandwich. Then the three of us put our heads together to figure out how I can make more money:

1. Find more magic show gigs.

2. Have a bake sale. (This could work . . . if it doesn't involve actual baking.)

3. Break open Freddy's Darth Vader bank and "borrow" his money. (This was Brian's idea and he was joking. I think.)

4. Ask my grandparents for a loan.

5. *Beg* my grandparents for a loan.

"Hey! Maybe you could sell one of your brothers," Brian says.

"Nah. I'd have to *pay* somebody to take Freddy."

"How about Jake? Lots of people want babies," Daniel says.

"Only perfect ones," Brian says.

Our table gets very quiet. I can't be positive, but I think Daniel kicks Brian under the table.

"Sorry," Brian says. "I didn't mean . . ."

"S'okay," I say.

"Anyway, you're wrong," Daniel tells Brian. "If people only want perfect babies, why did your parents keep you?"

We all laugh, except it's not *that* funny. Luckily, the bell rings and we head our separate ways for the next class.

I spend the rest of school still worrying about funding my trip. After English class, while I help Ms. Carlin rearrange some desks, I tell her I'm going to Magic Fest.

"That's amazing, Ethan! You must be thrilled!" She smiles, sharing my excitement.

I smile back and start talking a mile a minute. "I am. And I already know what I'm going to do for the close-up part. And Tina—Jake's babysitter?—is making a costume for my performance. But between figuring out how to get the money so I can actually go and coming up with an act for the main part of the competition, I've got a ton of stuff to do. Plus, I haven't even decided on a stage name yet." I stop to take a breath.

"It does sound overwhelming." Ms. Carlin puts her right hand under her chin, the way she always does when she's thinking. "Do you have time for some brainstorming?"

"Absolutely!"

She takes a chair and I grab another and we sit across from each other. "Okay," she says. "Let's start with what your act is about," she suggests.

"It's not really *about* anything. There's sight gags, juggling, sleight of hand—"

"Wow. Sounds like you have a lot going on."

"Is that good or bad?"

She tilts her head as she thinks about it. "Well, if there's no unifying theme, maybe that *is* your theme."

"How do you mean?"

"If your routine is chaotic, play up the chaos. Make it deliberate."

"Like, jump from one thing to the next on purpose?"

She nods. "Exactly. The absent-minded professor approach. You have a wonderful sense of humor. Why not use it as part of your act?"

After some more serious brainstorming, we come up with the perfect name for my act: The King of Chaos!

I spend the whole walk home repeating the name of my act in my head. The more I think about it, the more I like it.

Most magicians my age take themselves pretty seriously. If I can pull off a funny act, it might be different enough from the competition to win!

———————————

I walk in the front door to find Jake in his Kid Kart watching Tina move a penlight back and forth. I go over and squeeze his hands.

"Are you working hard?" I ask. Jake answers with one of his big toothy grins.

"He sure is," Tina says. "So far we—"

"Ethan, look!" Freddy hops into the room, interrupting as usual. He's holding a purple-and-yellow plastic cube. He hits one side and a flute plays classical music. He hits another and a harp plays a different piece. He brings it over and we check it out together.

"This is pretty cool," I say.

"The vision teacher brought it for Jake while we were at school," Freddy says.

Every week there's a new gadget that lights up, vibrates, or makes noise so Jake will try to reach out and grab it. Unfortunately, Freddy's the one who grabs the toys; all Jake grabs is Mom's long, curly hair. She always sits in on therapy sessions, so she can work with Jake the rest of the week, and tell us what to do, too. (Mom loves telling us what to do.)

I suddenly realize she's not around, which is strange. "Where's Mom?" I ask.

"She's not feeling so great," Tina tells me. "She had to lie down."

It's hard to imagine anyone sleeping through Freddy's noise, so I go down the hall and peek in my parents' room. Mom's awake, but her face is pale and her eyelids are droopy.

"Hi, sweetie." She gives me a sleepy smile. It's weird to see her lying down; she's usually running around doing ten things at once. "How was your day?"

"Great!" I plop down onto her bed. "Ms. Carlin and I—"

"Honey, don't get too close. I don't know if I'm contagious."

I stand and move to the door, while Mom shimmies into a sitting position. "Okay. Now tell me," she says.

"We came up with a name for my magic act: The King of Chaos."

She smiles. "I love it. Maybe you can . . ." Before she can finish the sentence, she has a coughing fit.

"Can I bring you some medicine or tea or something?"

She shakes her head and holds up a finger until she stops coughing. "There is one thing you could do."

"What?"

"Could you please stretch Jake for me after Tina leaves?"

I know it sounds strange to "stretch" someone, but since

Jake can't exercise on his own, we take turns moving his arms and legs up and down and in and out, a few times a day so they don't get too stiff. The therapists say it makes him feel better.

I tell Mom I'll take care of Jake and that she shouldn't worry. She thanks me, then closes her eyes.

I shut her door and go to my room: homework, then Jake, then Magic Fest prep! The more I read about Magic Fest, the more excited I am. There are magic shows, workshops on card tricks, lectures on staging with one-on-one coaching . . . and even a pizza party.

The main event, though, is the competition. There are three parts: the first is a close-up act with only a few people watching along with the judges; the second is on a big stage, where you perform in front of the judges and the other magicians; and finally, after both of those parts are scored, the top five magicians perform a second time. The winner gets five hundred dollars, plus the real prize: meeting and performing with Magnus the Magnificent!

Since I promised to keep my grades up, I force myself to concentrate on homework. As I read about magnets, I squeeze my red rubber ball in each hand for strength. While I memorize French verbs, I practice shuffling a deck of cards single-handed. Being a lefty, I'm pretty good with that hand, but my right's still giving me trouble.

By the time I've finished my English homework, Tina is long gone, Freddy's watching cartoons, and I still can't shuffle with my right hand. I take the deck with me and go to Jake's room.

He's wide awake, ready to hang out. I pull him into a sitting position, then grab some red crinkly paper, as noisy as it is shiny, and help him squeeze it. He smiles like nothing could be more fun. Maybe for him, nothing is.

After a couple minutes, I put him in the blue plastic chair on the floor and sit across from him. "Jake, I've got a problem. I can shuffle with two hands or only my left." I pull a deck of cards out of my pocket and show him. "I just can't do it with my right." I demonstrate and cards fly everywhere. I try again, and again . . . until I can't stand it anymore.

"I've been working on this for weeks! What do you think? Should I forget it?"

He looks at me with his calm blue eyes, and I look right back at him. I think about how hard he works with his therapists, how he never stops trying. I can almost hear him say, "Don't give up, Ethan. You can do it!"

I take a deep breath and let half the deck fall into my right palm. Then, slowly, carefully, I slip my finger underneath and push the bottom cards over the top ones.

"I did it! I finally did it!" I do it again and again. "We did it, Super Jake, you and me. The best team ever!" I pull him into my lap and move his arms back and forth crazy fast. He grins and grins. "Let's try some other decks." I take my *Lord of the Rings* cards out next and introduce him to Frodo, Merry, Pippin, and Sam.

"Hey there." Dad sticks his head in Jake's room. "Mom said you were working with Jake. Have you finished?"

Oh no! We were having so much fun I forgot to stretch him! "He only woke up a minute ago. I'll start now."

Dad shakes his head. "We'll have to skip it. He needs to eat—and so do we. I stopped by the pizza place Freddy likes. Could you put Jake in the Kid Kart while I get his food ready?"

I lift up Jake, strap him into the Kid Kart, and put in the tray while he watches me.

"I know," I tell him. "I shouldn't have lied. But the last thing I want is to upset Mom and Dad, especially after they agreed to let me go to Magic Fest and everything. You understand, right?" I squeeze his hands and he smiles, and I know he's not mad at me.

He never is.

CHAPTER TWELVE

It's amazing how even the *possibility* of meeting Magnus the Magnificent makes life, in general, better.

Like this morning, when Freddy helps himself to the last bowl of good cereal and I get stuck with oatmeal, I eat every spoonful without my usual complaint.

When Mom says, "Don't forget you have a trumpet lesson today, so come straight home after school," I tell her that's fine, even though I want to show Ms. Carlin my one-handed shuffle.

And when Betty the Crossing Guard asks how I'm doing, I smile and say I'm doing great. And I am . . . until gym class.

Ned and I are stuck as partners again. Whenever Mr. Davis isn't watching, Ned throws the basketball so high I'd need stilts to catch it. After about ten times, I finally say, "Hey, could you maybe throw it a little lower?"

I watch him scan the gym, probably to make sure the teacher isn't looking. Then he hurls it at my feet. Hard. I jump out of the way, then chase after the ball.

Eventually Mr. Davis blows his whistle, and it's finally time for my favorite thing: practicing foul shots. We each take ten shots in a row. For each one missed, you have to do five sit-ups.

I hate sit-ups so I make sure I don't miss.

I'm nine for nine and on my last shot. I take a deep breath, hold it, bounce the ball three times for luck like always, and—

"Break a leg!" Ned shouts.

I miss.

"Dammit!" I cry, then immediately wish I hadn't.

"Ooh, Ethan said a bad word," Ned says with a smirk.

Mr. Davis has a thing about swearing (though he's known to yell a few choice words himself every now and then). "On the floor, Ethan. That's five sit-ups for the missed shot and five more for profanity."

As much as I hate sit-ups, I hate Ned even more.

Luckily, my good mood comes back during lunch, and the rest of the day goes by super fast—even math class. (Miss Wright is out sick and the world's nicest sub does tonight's homework with us.)

I make it home right as the rain starts to fall, and five minutes later I'm under the carport. Freddy settles into the back of the minivan, I buckle Jake into his car seat, Mom clicks on the windshield wipers, and we're off to my trumpet lesson.

I'm just starting to tell Freddy and Jake a new Food Island story when Mom says, "Isn't that Ned?"

I look out the window and, sure enough, Ned's walking in the pouring rain. Before I can answer, Mom pulls over and opens her window.

"Hi," she says. "Remember me? I was at your house the other day. Your mom and I are—"

"I know who you are," Ned says without a smile.

I can see what's coming, and there's not a thing I can do about it.

"Would you like a ride?" Mom asks as he stands there getting drenched.

He shakes his head. "That's okay."

"It's no trouble," Mom says. "We're going right past your street."

And just like that, Ned's trapped. And so am I.

She unlocks the front passenger door and he climbs in.

"Hi, Ned!" Freddy-the-Traitor calls from the back seat. Ned turns around. His eyes glance my way . . . then settle on Jake. He stares at my brother a little too long.

"Did you miss your bus?" Mom asks.

He turns around and nods his head.

Mom tries to be friendly, asking typical, boring parent-type questions. After a bunch of one-word answers, she finally gives up. I don't bother saying anything to him and even Freddy is quiet for a change. I start wondering why just as I hear a *pop!* from behind me. I turn around and see a ginormous pink bubble splattered all over Freddy's nose and cheeks.

"Oops," he says.

After what seems like a thousand years, we pull up in front of Ned's house and he gets out.

"Thanks for the ride," he mumbles.

"Anytime," Mom says with a smile. He walks toward his house without glancing back.

As we drive away, my shoulders finally relax, and I exhale loudly.

"Poor thing," Mom says.

Huh?

"Rox says he really misses Chicago. His dad's still there, you know. It must be hard being away from him."

Whatever.

"It's not easy being the new kid at school. Rox says he hasn't made a lot of friends yet."

There's a shocker.

"She and I were hoping you two could . . ."

Nope. Don't even say it . . .

"... be friends. Maybe you could invite him over sometime and—"

"No," I say.

"Why not?"

There are so many reasons, I don't know where to start, so I decide to keep it simple. "We don't get along."

Something in my voice must convince her it's the truth, because she doesn't push the issue. We ride in silence for a minute or two, then I get back to the Food Island story and finish it exactly as we reach my trumpet teacher's house.

CHAPTER THIRTEEN

I love weekends. It's a shame they only last for two days. It would be so much better if school was two days and weekends were five.

One of my favorite things about the weekend is that I can sleep late—at least, in theory....

"Ethan? Are you awake?" Mom asks outside my room.

I am now.

When she cracks open my door, she's got on the biggest smile I've seen in weeks.

"Your brother has a playdate," she says, like it's the best thing in the world.

"Um, okay?"

"You should come see."

"Why? I've seen Freddy and Tyler a million times—"

"Freddy and Tyler are out with your dad." Her smile gets

even bigger. "I'm talking about your *other* brother."

I clamber out of bed and follow her down the hall, into the kitchen.

Jake's in his Kid Kart with eyes open wide, watching Wendy pour invisible tea into miniature pink and purple teacups. She adds imaginary sugar cubes with an impossibly tiny spoon and gently places a cup on his tray.

"Careful," Wendy tells him. "Hot!" She blows on his cup and lifts it to his lips.

Jake has found a friend.

Around half an hour later, the four of us pile into the minivan to take advantage of a warm November day, and go to a playground half an hour away. There's nothing wrong with the ones nearby; they just aren't for kids like Jake. This one has ramps everywhere and colorful, super-big pieces of equipment that everyone can use.

Like we do every time we visit this playground, we start with the swings. I help Mom strap Jake into a big red swing. It's got a really deep bucket seat so kids who can't sit up on their own can still use it. There's even a swing sturdy enough to hold someone in a wheelchair. Mom pushes Jake while I push Wendy in a regular swing right next to him.

Next, we go into this gigantic glider that can hold six or

eight people (half on each side), plus a wheelchair in the middle. Mom sits with Wendy and another kid, while I hold Jake on my lap on the other side, and a dad pushes us back and forth. Then I get out and push, so the dad can sit with his little boy.

After that, Mom and I take turns holding Jake real tight and going down an extra-wide slide, while Wendy uses a second slide next to us. Then we go to one of the picnic benches and I spread snacks out on the table while Mom gets Jake's food ready. I can tell Mom made a special effort to make Jake's food as close to ours as possible. I don't know if Wendy notices (and I'm pretty sure Jake doesn't), but it makes me happy.

While Mom feeds Jake mushy banana out of a jar, Wendy and I eat the kind you peel. When Jake eats baby custard, Wendy and I eat pudding cups and Mom snacks on yogurt. And when we drink apple juice, Jake does, too. I smile at Mom. "I like this picnic a lot," I tell her.

"Me too," she says. And she smiles back.

On the ride home, I tell knock-knock jokes and Wendy giggles, and when Mom plays little kids' songs on the CD player, Wendy sings along. It's pretty cute, and I'm glad Wendy likes the jokes and music. I hope Jake does, too.

When we get back home, Mom puts Jake to bed, and Wendy passes out in the big purple recliner. Mom and I sit on the sofa, keeping an eye on Wendy. Since Freddy's still away with Tyler and Dad, we start plotting which *Star Wars* presents to get Freddy for Hanukkah. It's still a few weeks away, but Mom always likes to plan ahead.

The longer we talk, the sillier our ideas get.

"How 'bout a life-size R2-D2?" I suggest.

Mom laughs. "Why not a life-size Chewbacca?"

"Can you picture him in the minivan?"

Mom squeezes her lips and squints, like she's thinking really hard. "We'll have to get the *Millennium Falcon*, too," she says. "Think it'll fit in our carport?"

"Maybe if . . ." I break off as a car pulls into our driveway.

"It's Rox," Mom says.

"I'll get it." I open the door, and Rox flies into the room.

"I'm so sorry I'm late! Ned's appointment ran over and—"

At the sound of her mom's voice, Wendy's eyes open wide. "Mommy!"

"Hey, princess." Rox scoops her daughter into her arms. "Did you have fun with Jake?"

"I love him," Wendy announces.

Mom smiles. "They had a wonderful time together. Your tea set was a big hit."

"Here's to the next generation of friends," Rox says.

Wendy tugs on her mom's shirt. "Mommy, I'm thirsty."

"I've got plenty of milk and juice boxes. . . ." Mom gives Rox a knowing smile. "Not to mention an endless supply of hazel-nut coffee and . . ."

Rox smiles back. "You had me at hazelnut." She and Wendy follow Mom to the kitchen table. "Maybe I can finally meet Jake."

"You haven't met him yet?" I ask.

"Your dad was giving him a bath when I dropped Wendy off," Rox says.

"Why don't you go see if he's awake?" Mom asks me, then she scurries around, grabbing cookies and cups and saucers and plates that match, and even the butterfly sugar bowl she only brings out for special occasions.

I go down the hall and, sure enough, Jake's wide awake. I lift him into the Kid Kart, buckle him in, and attach the tray. "Hey, Jake. Wendy's mom wants to meet you. Try to make a good first impression, for Mom's sake." I squeeze his hands, and he smiles at me.

"This coffee is amazing," Rox says as Jake and I enter the room.

"Jake!" Wendy forgets her half-eaten cookie and runs over to him.

Rox holds her coffee cup in midair. Her smile sort of freezes.

Mom smooths Jake's curls. "This is Jake."

Rox puts down her cup. "Hi, Jake."

Wendy helps Jake wave. "He says hi back."

Rox sort of waves, too.

Wendy skips back to her seat and takes another bite of cookie.

Rox takes one from the box. "Wendy, maybe Jake would like one?"

Wendy shakes her head. "He can't eat cookies," she says, crumbs flying out of her mouth.

"Oh," Rox says. "Maybe a glass of milk?"

Wendy shakes her head again.

Rox takes a deep breath, then another sip of coffee.

"I'll warm a bottle for him." Mom heads for the fridge.

"You know . . ." Rox stands. "We really should be going."

Mom stops in her tracks. "This'll just take a minute, promise."

"No, we . . . I need to get home and start dinner."

I look at the clock: it's 3:45 p.m.

Mom's shoulders slump. "Oh, well, if you're sure."

"I am. Thanks so much for . . . we'll do it again soon. My house next time."

"Sounds good," Mom says.

"Bye-bye, Jake," Wendy says.

I help him wave goodbye.

———————————

A few hours later, Jake's pretend tea is replaced with a bowl of real applesauce and the rest of us are chowing down on one of our favorite meals: spaghetti. Even Jake likes it. He's tried about a dozen sauces by now and likes the ones without green peppers best. Dad puts on Italian music, Mom lights long red candles, and Freddy and I play a game we like to call "Who can swallow the longest noodle?"

Mom invented a game, too. She calls it "Who has the most sauce on his clothes?" The "winner" washes the dishes. Spoiler alert: it's always Freddy.

Dinner is great, but while Mom and Dad talk about their days and Freddy splatters sauce all over himself, I keep thinking about Wendy and Jake's tea party.

"Ethan, is something on your mind?" Mom asks as she serves up more pasta. "You seem preoccupied."

"I was just thinking. Jake's birthday is coming up, and now that he's got a friend . . . maybe we could have a party for him and invite Wendy."

"And Mandy!" Freddy pipes up. "She can give him whipped cream."

"That's a wonderful idea!" Mom says. "We'll invite Wendy, and Jake's therapists, and Tina, and the Group . . ."

Dad passes the garlic bread. "Sounds like a lot of work, Bec," he tells Mom.

"Will there be cake? And ice cream?" Freddy asks.

"It's not a party otherwise," Mom answers.

"I love parties!" Freddy jumps up, spilling what's left on his plate all over his shirt. "Oops."

After the dishes (and Freddy) get cleaned up, we create a guest list, a menu, and even a game to play for Jake's birthday party. Then I read another chapter of *Merlin* to Mom and Freddy while Dad gets Jake ready for bed. We're at this really intense part where Merlin is trapped inside a stone. He can't move, talk, see, or hear, but he's still himself. He's still Merlin.

Later, when I go in to say good night to Jake, Bugs Bunny is holding an envelope with my name on it. "Hey, what's this?" I squeeze Jake's hands, and he smiles at me. I open the envelope, pull out a piece of paper, and read it out loud:

Dear Ethan,

Mommy said I should go to sleep, but I'm too excited about my party—and it was all your idea!

I wanted to do something nice for you, too. So Mommy and Daddy and I came up with something we think you'll like.

Love, Jake

I see a second envelope next to Tweety Bird. Inside, there's a printed ticket that reads MAGIC FEST REGISTRATION: ONE JUNIOR MAGICIAN!

Mom and Dad walk in, grinning at me.

"I can't believe it!" I hug them tight, then hug Jake, too. "Thank you *so* much!"

"What happened?" Freddy runs in, his mouth brimming over with frothy toothpaste.

I'm so excited, I give him a hug, too, and don't even care that toothpaste splatters all over my shirt.

CHAPTER FOURTEEN

As usual, the weekend went by too fast and Monday is here before I know it. It's usually hard waking up for school, but today I wake up even earlier than I have to, so before school I can eat breakfast and still have time to count the money I've been saving up. Now that the registration fee is covered, I might actually be able to pay for the rest of the trip. . . .

I cover my bed with the money I've saved so far: twenty-dollar bills, a pile of quarters, and everything in between. Katie's party is coming up soon; plus, two more are scheduled on the calendar. If I'm lucky, some parents will feel generous and tip me—or book me for their own kid's party.

I put everything back into the bank Bubba gave me. It's shaped like a top hat, with a slot to drop money into on top. It was originally see-through, but I didn't want anyone (meaning Freddy) to see how much money was in it, so Tina covered it with silver glitter and now it's even more awesome (and more private).

I head to the living room, where Mom and Jake are having a joint session with Mandy and Suzette. Suzette is one of Jake's physical therapists. Her job is to try to help Jake move better. She's got a French accent and is really good friends with Mandy. The funny thing is, Mandy wants Jake to eat more, and Suzette wants him to eat less. She says if he gains too much weight, it'll be even harder for him to roll over or sit up.

"Bonjour, Ethan!" Suzette smiles at me. She's holding Jake facedown on top of a big green ball. Mandy's sitting on the floor in front of him, squeezing a bright red plastic chicken. They're hoping Jake will try to lift his head to see it.

"Bonjour, Suzette." I grab my backpack and open the door before I run out of French conversation.

"Have a good day!" Mom calls as I head out.

And it is a good day . . . until gym class.

Once again, I'm paired with my favorite teammate. He's in a worse mood than usual, for whatever reason. If he weren't so obnoxious, I'd almost feel bad for him, with his dad in Chicago and everything.

"You throw like a girl," he says, snarling in my direction.

"Some *girls* throw better than you. Your little sister, for example," I say jokingly.

"You think you're real smart, don't you?"

I smile, determined not to let him get to me. "Is that a rhetorical question?"

He throws the ball hard, but I catch it. "The only reason everyone's nice to you," he says, "is because your dad's the assistant principal."

I throw the ball back, hoping Mr. Davis will blow his whistle and we can move on to foul shots or something.

Ned takes a step closer. "Your dad's a joke."

"Your dad's in Chicago." I blurt it out before even realizing what I said.

Ned's face turns red, and I instantly regret my words. Before I can think of a way to take them back, he says, "Your brother's a retard!"

Just then, Mr. Davis blows his whistle, signaling us to line up for foul shots. I know I should move, but I don't. I know I should ignore Ned, but I can't. And I know I should keep my mouth shut.

But I won't.

It's one thing to pick on me, or even my dad. But Jake is off-limits.

"He has brain damage. What's your excuse?" I shout at Ned.

"I bet your dad wishes Jake had never been born." Ned takes a step closer to me. "I bet you all do."

My fingers grip the ball. Tight. "SHUT UP!"

"Make me."

My hands let go of the ball then fly up to Ned's chest and shove him. He's a lot taller and heavier than I am, but my anger is stronger and takes us both by surprise. He falls backward and I lunge toward him, swinging my fists.

Everyone's gathered around, watching us and shouting: "Fight! Fight!"

"Break it up!" Mr. Davis's voice is like thunder. "Ethan! That's enough!"

My hands drop to my sides and my breath comes hard and fast, like I just ran a marathon.

"Are you all right?" Mr. Davis asks. I start to answer, but he's not talking to me. As he pulls Ned from the floor, Ned nods but doesn't take his eyes off me.

After that everything is a blur. Nothing feels real. I can't believe I got into a fight. I can't believe how happy I was just last night, or how happy my parents were with me. So happy they even paid for my Magic Fest registration.

I can't even imagine how *un*happy they'll be now, or how much trouble I'll be in. I wish there were a trapdoor I could escape through. . . .

I've been sitting in the office for half an hour now, wishing everything would disappear. I shut my eyes, but I still see Ned on the ground, looking up at me. And I still see the expression on Dad's face when he was called out of a meeting . . . because of me. He looked as stunned as I felt—as I feel.

At first, no one knew what to do with me, then it was decided that someone other than Dad would deal with me at school, since it would be all kinds of awkward for him to discipline me here. So, the other assistant principal gave me a lecture and said, since this was my "first offense" and there were "extraneous circumstances," I wouldn't be suspended or get detention or anything.

I have a feeling I won't get off so easily at home.

By the time everything was sorted out, fourth period had already started, but there was no way I'd be able to concentrate in class. I didn't want to stay at school another second. All I wanted was to go home and take a nap. A really long nap. So I called Mom to pick me up. . . .

"Ethan?"

I open my eyes and there she is, standing over me. Her face is all scrunched up and worried, but this time it's all because of me.

"Are you all right?"

"I guess. Did Dad call you, too?"

She nods. "He had to go to a meeting, so he couldn't give me all the details."

Which makes me wonder exactly what details he *did* give her. Will she be mad at me or be on my side?

"Let's go." She touches my arm. "Jake was sleeping, so Chris's mom is watching him 'til we get back."

Five minutes later, we're home. Mom thanks Mrs. Todd, who says Jake is still sleeping, then she walks across the street to her house and it's just the two of us. I tell Mom what happened. She listens quietly, not interrupting even once. When I finally finish, I feel better that the story's out, but I'm worried about what she'll say. So I take a deep breath and ask, "What do you think? Was I wrong to stand up for Jake?"

"Well . . ."

Just then, her phone rings. I can't believe it. She glances at the screen.

"It's Emma," she says. "I'll just be a minute. . . ."

I decide to visit Jake, in case he's awake. Luckily, he is. I lower the railing on his bed (which is there, even though he never rolls over anyway) and squeeze his hands.

"Hey, Jake." He smiles at me. I can't smile back. "You won't believe what happened. I got into this huge fight with Ned and now everything's all messed up."

He looks at me with those big blue eyes of his. I know he's listening, and I know he understands. Sometimes I think he's the only one who does. Mom comes in and scoops Jake into a hug, then sits down and holds him in her lap.

"Join us." She pats the space next to her, and I sit on the little bed. "I think you were right to speak up for Jake," Mom says, "and I'm proud of you."

I feel *so* much better.

"But fighting is not how our family solves things. Ethan, you know better than that!"

"You and Dad always say I should look out for my brothers. What was I supposed to do? Let Ned say mean stuff about Jake?"

"Of course not. You could have talked to me about it instead."

"I *am* talking to you."

"It's a little late." She gives me a half smile. "Listen. I'm not going to sit here and excuse what Ned said. The thing is, it sounds like he was trying to provoke you—and you let him."

"I know. I was there."

She looks away from me and pulls Jake in close for a hug.

"Sorry," I say. "I know you're trying to help."

"I am." She leans over and gives me a hug, too. "There just isn't a whole lot I can do at this point."

I hug her back. It's nice to know one of my parents isn't mad at me.

I'm not so sure about the other.

CHAPTER FIFTEEN

It's only the middle of the afternoon, but I guess the day has caught up with me. Mom gets Jake ready for his bath and I go to my room, fall into bed, and pull the blanket over my head.

I must have dozed off, because when Freddy opens my door I'm completely disoriented—then it all comes rushing back: the fight with Ned, Mom picking me up at school, the look on Dad's face. . . .

"Whatcha doin'?" Freddy asks.

"Trying to sleep," I tell him from under the blanket.

"Mommy and I are working on the jigsaw puzzle! Wanna help?"

"No." I wait until he leaves, then throw off the blanket, turn on the light, and stare at my David Copperfield, Houdini, and Magnus posters, doing my best to channel their amazingness. Nothing less will get me out of this mess.

"Guess what?" You-know-who bursts into my space. Again.

"I'm busy."

He crinkles his nose. "Doing what? Invisible homework?" He laughs at his dumb joke. "Guess what Mommy's gonna let Jakey try for dessert tonight?"

"Sushi."

"Nope. Wanna guess again?"

"No."

"A Popsicle! Guess what flavor?"

"If I get it right, will you leave me alone?"

He's quiet for a full three seconds, which means he's thinking. Hard. "Okay."

"Cherry."

"How did you know?"

"He liked the cherry lollipop last week." I wiggle my fingers. "See ya."

He leaves. Again.

I grab a piece of paper and write HOW TO GET OUT OF THIS MESS. Then I start a list under it:

1. Be sure Mom talks to Dad, but first, remind her how proud she was I stood up for Jake.

2. Talk to Emma and Bubba in case they know how I can get out of this mess.

3. Try talking to Dad.

I think about that one for a minute or two, then add: If he's not too mad.

4. Make up for the fight by getting all A's on my
   report card.

Right. Good luck with that. Before I come up with the next idea, my door opens for the third time. "Go away, Freddy."

Only it's not Freddy. It's Dad. And he does *not* look happy. He looks so not happy that my stomach starts to hurt and I want to go back to bed and pull the covers over my head again. He closes the door and sits on my bed.

"Ethan, we need to talk," he says.

"I know." I put my pencil down.

"Why don't you go first and tell me what happened?"

I try to talk, but I don't know what to say. I try to swallow, but my mouth is dry. "I don't know where to start."

Dad rubs his forehead the way he always does when he's upset but doesn't want us to know it. "It's usually best to start at the beginning. Why did you get into a fight with Ned?"

"'Cause he made me mad."

Dad shakes his head. "People get mad every day. But they don't start—"

"He called Jake a retard!"

Suddenly, it's like someone hit the pause button. After a few seconds, Dad lets out a long breath. "I'm sorry he said that."

I can tell he's trying to figure out what to say next.

"Sometimes when people are upset they say things they don't mean, and we have to . . . move past it."

"Move past it?"

"Sometimes we have to be the bigger person and try to understand where the other person is coming from."

"I *understood* him just fine."

Dad speaks softly but his disappointment comes through loud and clear. "That's no excuse for shoving him."

"He started it!"

"And you can end it."

"But he—"

Dad puts his hand up, stopping me midsentence. "You need to apologize."

I exhale. "I'm sorry."

"Not to me. To Ned."

"You're kidding, right?"

Dad stands up, looking more angry than unhappy. "Do I look like I'm kidding?"

"What about Jake?"

"This isn't about Jake." He massages the back of his neck.

"Sure it is!" I stand up, too. "You're always saying we should stand up for each other. But *you* won't stand up for *me*! Or Jake . . ."

Something in his face changes. The anger leaves, and he just looks . . . like Dad. He walks over and puts his hand on my shoulder. "I will always stand up for Jake. And for you. But there are better ways to stand up for someone than getting into a fist fight."

I open my mouth to argue some more, but he keeps talking. "You know as well as I do our school has a strict no-fighting policy."

"I know, but—"

"I understand that Ned may have started the fight with his words."

"'May have'? He totally did!"

"But you threw the first punch."

I open my mouth to argue some more, only Dad doesn't give me the chance. "Enough," he says, his voice soft but firm. "You need to apologize to Ned."

"He should apologize to me! And to Jake." My voice is just as firm.

"I'm sorry, Ethan. If you don't apologize to him, Magic Fest is off."

No. Not that. Anything but that.

It feels like my heart has stopped beating.

"I'm asking one last time. Tell him you're sorry, and this all goes away."

Maybe he's right. It's just two words. Say I'm sorry and everything's forgiven. We'll all act like nothing happened, and I can go to Magic Fest and everything is okay again.

Except it's not.

It's not forgiven and it's not forgotten and it isn't going away because what Ned said is *not* okay.

I reach inside my desk drawer, pull out the Magic Fest registration, and hand it over.

I don't know if a few minutes, or a few hours, go by. And I don't know what I'm going to do if I can't go to Magic Fest. But I know one thing: nobody makes fun of Jake.

I won't let them.

I open my bedroom door, slip down the hallway, and enter Jake's room to see how he's doing. Mom is already there, playing with him inside "the Little Room," this three-sided box with all sorts of stuff to touch and look at.

"Dad said I could go to Magic Fest and that everything would be okay if I tell Ned I'm sorry."

Mom lets go of the shiny silver beads hanging over Jake's left hand and turns to me. I can see by the sad look in her eyes that she already knows what I decided. "Oh, sweetie . . ." She reaches out and puts her hand on mine.

"What Ned said . . . I can't pretend it's okay." I touch Jake's little foot with my other hand and hold on to it. "No matter what."

Mom squeezes my hand. "I am so sorry this happened. I know how much Magic Fest means to you."

There's more I want to say, but the knot in my throat makes it hard to say it. I grab the yellow flashlight and shine it on the red foil over Jake's head.

"Is there anything I can do to help?" she asks.

"You could tell Dad to let me go."

"Ethan . . ."

"I was only sticking up for Jake."

She rolls Jake onto his right side and shakes the silver beads for him to look at. "Dad knows that. I'm afraid it's more complicated, though."

I hate it when adults say things are complicated. If something is complicated, it's usually because *they* make it that way. Ned making fun of Jake? "Seems pretty *un*complicated to me: he was a jerk and I stood up for my brother. What's so complicated?"

Mom sighs. "Ethan, your dad is the assistant principal. He can't condone anyone fighting—especially his own son."

"Ned started it," I say for what feels like the umpteenth time.

She stops jingling the beads and looks at me. "Listen. Ned's parents have been divorced less than a year. It's been really tough on him."

I roll my eyes. "Lots of kids have divorced parents. They don't act like he does."

"Maybe not. But his dad's in a different state, his grades have fallen, and he's got this adorable little sister who can do no wrong."

I slide a filter over the flashlight and it turns the Little Room red. "Just because things are hard doesn't give him the right to be mean—especially to Jake."

Mom rolls Jake onto his other side so he can see himself in the mirror. "You're absolutely right." She helps him squeeze a little orange ball that squeaks. "Still. I can't help feeling sorry for Ned."

"Well, I feel sorry for *me*. It's not like my life is so great, either."

Mom puts the ball down and looks at me like I just said the worst thing ever. I stare at a piece of crinkly paper on the floor so I don't have to look at the hurt expression on her face.

"I'm sorry you feel that way." Her voice is soft and sad.

I sigh. "What I meant was—"

"I know exactly what you meant." She gently scoops Jake out of the Little Room and into her arms, hugging him tight as his eyes start to close.

"I realize our life isn't easy," she says. "But at least we all have each other."

She puts Jake in his bed for a nap and leaves the room. I head toward the kitchen to get a glass of water. Dad and Freddy are in the living room watching TV. They both laugh at the same time, and Freddy squeezes in under Dad's arm, fitting perfectly like a piece in a jigsaw puzzle . . . just like I used to.

I wonder if Ned used to sit that way with his dad, too.

CHAPTER SIXTEEN

"Seriously? *You* pushed *Ned?*" Brian asks in between French fries.

"Yeah, that's pretty wild." Daniel dumps ketchup on his last bite of hot dog. "Sucks about Magic Fest."

"Tell me about it." I have no appetite, so I slide my lunch tray toward him.

"You can't give up." Daniel bites into my turkey sandwich. "There's gotta be something you can do to get back into the competition."

"If you think of it, let me know."

"Well, at least winter break starts soon," Brian says. "And now you don't have to spend it working on your magic act."

Great. A hollow feeling spreads inside me, and I don't think it's going away any time soon.

"What he means"—Daniel shoots Brian a dirty look—"is

there will be tons of other chances."

"Not to meet Magnus." I crumple my brown paper bag.

Daniel says, "I get where you're coming from. All you did was stick up for Jake. It isn't fair you're being punished for it."

I shrug. "Doesn't matter anymore. It's over."

What's not over is the rest of school. I consider going to the nurse; I really *am* feeling sick. But she'd call Mom and Mom would have to stop whatever she's doing with Jake, and I already called her to get me yesterday. . . . Besides, it's not like I'll feel any better at home, with my magician posters and magic props everywhere. Even Miss Wright and math equations can't make me feel any worse.

I slog through the rest of my classes. When the final bell rings, I barely have the energy to load my backpack.

"Ethan?" Ms. Carlin walks over to my desk. "I heard you and Ned got into a fight. Do you want to talk about it?"

I shrug.

She turns a chair around so we're facing each other and sits. "Sometimes it helps to talk things out. But only if you want."

I sigh then say, "Ned called Jake a bad name, and my dad got mad at *me* because I pushed Ned, and now I can't go to Magic Fest because I won't apologize for sticking up for my little brother."

"My goodness. That's a lot to process. I'm going to need a moment." She gets up, goes to her desk, and pulls something out. "I might need this, too." She brings over a chocolate bar, breaks it in half, and gives me the bigger piece.

"Thanks." I take a bite. It's really good, and for the first time all day, I'm starting to feel better.

"Ethan, it's not like you to get in trouble. What happened right before the name calling?"

I've been trying to forget the whole thing, so it takes a minute to remember. "Ned called my dad a loser."

"That must have upset you. Then what happened?"

"I said *his* dad was in Chicago." Suddenly the chocolate doesn't taste as good.

Ms. Carlin looks confused.

"His parents are divorced. He said something mean about my dad, so . . ."

"You retaliated by doing the same."

I nod. It's much easier to stay mad at Ned when I forget that part.

She tilts her head a little. "If you could take back what you said, would you?"

"I wanted to right after I said it, but then he . . . you know."

"It's easier to say things in anger than it is to take them back," she says.

"Did Shakespeare write that?"

She smiles. "No. But, as you know, he did write, 'If you pardon, we will mend.'"

"So you're saying I should forgive Ned?"

"I'm saying that perhaps you should forgive each other. It's possible he regrets what he said, too."

Hmm. I never thought of that.

"Confucius said, 'To be wronged is nothing unless you continue to remember it.' Ethan, only *you* can decide if it's worth holding on to your anger."

On the way home I think about the anger I'm holding on to.

By the time I get home, I'm angry at *myself* for even thinking about forgiving Ned. He doesn't deserve it.

I open the door, put my trumpet case on the floor, and throw my backpack down super hard.

"Whoa!" Tina walks into the living room. "What did that backpack do to you?"

I shrug.

"C'mere, you old grouch."

I give her a half-hearted hug and she gives me a full-hearted one.

"Ethan!" Freddy races into the room, his lips covered in blue icing. "Guess what Tina and I made?"

"Something with blue icing?"

His eyes double in size. "Cupcakes! How'd you guess?"

Tina laughs and hands him a tissue. He wipes half of the blue goo away, then runs off to his room.

"So," she asks, "what's got you in such a jolly mood?"

I don't feel like getting into the whole Ned-made-fun-of-Jake-so-I-hit-him story again. "I don't wanna talk about it."

She shrugs. "Suit yourself. Hungry?"

I shake my head. "Where is everybody?"

"Jake had an awesome session with Suzette, so he's taking a nap. And your mom's visiting some friend who's obsessed with coffee."

Oh no. That's gotta be Rox. Since Jake is here and Wendy's there, it's not a playdate. Are Mom and Rox still friends after what happened with Ned and me? What if—

Tina waves her hand in front of my face. "Am I boring you?"

"Huh?"

"What is going on with you?"

"It's a long story. . . ."

She smiles. "Those are my favorite kind. Let me go check on your brothers, then you can tell me all about it."

She's still checking on Jake when I look out the living room window and see Mom pull into the carport. Before she puts her key in the door, Dad pulls up, too. They meet halfway and stand there, talking in the driveway. Mom's using her hands a lot and Dad's shaking his head and I wonder if I'm in even more trouble somehow.

Meanwhile, Tina carries Jake into the living room, and she's all smiles. Mom and Dad are *not* all smiles as they walk down the driveway together.

"Uh-oh," Tina says. "They don't look very happy."

I hear Mom's key in the door and try not to panic. After all, things can't get any worse.

"Hey," Tina says, looking at me. "I left something for you on your bed. Hope you like it."

"Thanks." Knowing her, it's either a comic book or a magazine article about Magnus. She's gonna feel really bad when I tell her Magic Fest is off.

Mom comes in and, as usual, fusses over Jake and listens while Tina reports on the afternoon, but she keeps looking over at me. I don't know what she's thinking, but I'm guessing it's not good.

Dad hangs up his coat, says hi to Tina and Jake, and barely glances in my direction before he goes down the hall. He's either upset or tired, or both.

Tina warms a bottle for Jake, brings it to Mom, and leaves.

"I saw Rox this afternoon," Mom says. She looks at me

and Jake looks at her as he drinks his bottle. "She feels terrible about what Ned said to you. She thinks he's the one who should apologize."

"She does? Did you tell Dad that?"

"I did."

"And?"

Mom pauses to rub Jake's back. The suspense is killing me. "This whole thing has really upset your father."

"Upset *him*? I'm the one who's not going to Magic Fest! All I did was stand up for Jake."

Mom opens her mouth to respond, then closes it again. I think that means she agrees with me, but doesn't want to say anything against Dad.

I look at Jake, who is contentedly drinking his bottle. He never has to make tough decisions and he never gets in trouble. No one ever gets mad at Jake.

I go to my room and turn on the light. There's a big bag on my bed: Tina's surprise. I open the bag and look inside. It's a purple velvet cape with glittery moons and stars all over it: my King of Chaos costume.

The longer I stare at it, the worse I feel. An ache starts in my stomach and goes straight to my heart. I stare so long at the cape that everything goes blurry. I wipe my eyes, put the costume back into the bag, and take it down the hall to my parents' room. Maybe if they see all the trouble Tina went to, they'll feel guilty and change their minds about Magic Fest.

I'm about to knock on the closed door when I hear Dad's muffled voice: "The rules clearly state that punishment is up to our discretion."

My hand stops midair. I stand as quietly as possible, barely breathing.

Mom's voice is next. "I agree one hundred percent. And I say missing Magic Fest is punishment enough."

"Becca, fighting is one of the most serious infractions in the parent handbook."

"I know," Mom answers. "I read it—particularly the part about *physically* harming another student. What about *emotionally* harming?"

I feel like cheering from the sidelines, but I stay silent. It's a good thing, too, because all of a sudden it's quiet on the other side of the door. Really quiet. I hold my breath and lean in closer so I don't miss anything.

After a few seconds, I hear Mom's voice again, soft but strong. "It's true Ethan threw the first *physical* punch, but we both know what Ned said was just as painful—probably more so."

More silence, then I hear Dad say, "All right. We'll leave it as is."

I thank Mom (silently, of course). Then I head back to my room to think about everything I just heard. It's only when I close my door that I realize I'm still holding the bag with my King of Chaos costume inside.

CHAPTER SEVENTEEN

"Is it today? Is it today?"

Without even opening my eyes, I know Freddy is bouncing up and down in his goofy snowman pajamas. He's been doing it every morning since Mom sent out invitations for Jake's birthday party.

The difference is, this time I open my eyes and say, "It *is* today!"

Jake's party is in the party room at our grandparents' condo. The five of us arrive early to get everything ready. Dad puts together a salad big enough for the *Guinness World Records,* while Mom stirs up a huge crockpot of homemade chili. Freddy pulls out his crayon box to make a HAPPY BIRTH-DAY, JAKE! sign, and I put together a plate of cheese, crackers, and grapes.

Meanwhile, Bubba tries every button on the party room's

mysterious coffee maker, and Emma sings "The Alphabet Song" to the guest of honor, who is sitting in her lap with one eye open and one eye closed. He's all dressed up in his brand-new Oscar the Grouch sweater.

"Anybody need some help?" a familiar voice calls out.

"Chris!" I stop building my tower of cheese and Freddy and I run to the door, practically tripping over each other to get to our favorite neighbor.

He lifts Freddy up and swings him around in a circle.

"Are you already done with school?" Freddy asks.

"I wish." Chris laughs, still spinning him around. "I'm home for winter break."

"You are so lucky," I tell him. "We have a whole week left."

"I feel your pain." Chris puts Freddy down, high-fives me, then goes over to Jake and squeezes his hands. "Hey, Jake. Happy birthday!"

Having Chris back puts all of us in an even happier mood—plus, he's really tall, so we get the streamers up a lot faster. So fast that there's time for Freddy and me to show him a new card trick before the other guests arrive.

I pull out a deck of cards from my jeans pocket. (Ethan's Rule #4: A good magician should always have a deck of cards available.) While Chris and Freddy chat, I shuffle the cards and put ten on the table.

"Okay," I tell Chris. "Look at these cards and choose one—but don't tell me which it is. Tell Freddy instead."

Chris picks a card and whispers into Freddy's ear.

"Now, Freddy will point to one card at a time and I'll tell you the one you chose."

"Sounds good," Chris says.

Freddy points to the ten of hearts. "Is that it?"

"Nope," I say.

He points to the three of diamonds. "Is that it?"

"Nope," I say again.

He points to the ace of spades. "Is that it?"

"That's it," I say.

Chris smiles. "Okay, let's do it again," he says.

This time, Freddy points to the right card on the second try. Then we do it a third time, and he points to the right card on the fifth try.

"Hmm," Chris says. "What if we try it with nine cards instead of ten?"

"No problem," I tell him. Because it isn't. It doesn't matter how many cards you use as long as you know how to use them. I'm shuffling the deck again when the other guests start showing up, so I promise to do the trick for him later with only nine cards.

Once everyone's arrived, there are about thirty people

crammed into the party room, including Dad's parents (who drove down from Pennsylvania), Chris's parents, Tina, Jake's therapists, Wendy and Rox, and "the Group." Seeing Rox makes me think about Ned, which is the last thing I want to do right now (or ever). I try my best to avoid making eye contact with her.

The first thing we do is play "Everything You Wanted to Know about Jake, but Were Afraid to Ask." It's sort of a test, only with funny questions, like:

Jake enjoys eating:
a) squash
b) peas
c) applesauce
d) everything

(If you guessed D, you get one point.)

Jake's guests fill out the quiz, occasionally stopping to write him a birthday message in a blank Winnie the Pooh book Mom passes around. Meanwhile, Dad is busy taking pictures of people smiling and laughing and hugging Jake, while Freddy pesters Chris with questions like, "Does your roommate like *Star Wars*?" and Wendy shows Jake a Disney princess book.

I stand in the corner, avoiding Rox and munching cheese.

I'm on my sixth piece when Bubba joins me. "Hey, buddy! Try to leave some cheese for the rest of us." He winks. "How about doing one of your magic tricks for me?"

Before I can even answer him, Pop-Pop, my other grandfather, ambles over. "Did I hear something about magic tricks?"

"How 'bout a card trick?" I start to pull my deck out again when I spot something I can use for a different kind of trick. "Actually, hold on a second."

I get Freddy's crayon box and hand five different-colored crayons to Bubba, then turn my back to him. "Choose any color you like and be sure to let Pop-Pop see it."

"Okay," Bubba says. "I choose orange."

I laugh. "You're not supposed to tell me! I'm supposed to guess. Choose again."

"Okay, buddy, I won't choose orange this time."

"Bubba!"

Pop-Pop laughs.

I sigh. Maybe I should've practiced on my grandmothers instead. I put my hands behind my back.

"All right, Bubba. Without saying *anything*, place the crayon in my hands."

He puts it in my right hand. I turn back to face my audience, holding it for a few more seconds, then bring my left—the empty one—in front of my face, concentrating hard.

"I'm sensing a bright, cheerful color. Is it . . . Bubba! You chose orange again!"

"That's pretty good, buddy!" Bubba grins. "I was trying to fool you."

I shake my head and laugh. "Okay, to make it even more challenging, I'm going to let *you* pick any five crayons you want." As I hand them a box of sixty-four colors, Freddy runs up.

"Hey! Are those my crayons?"

"I'll give them right back after this trick, okay?"

"Will you show me how it works?"

"No. But I'll let you choose the crayons."

He thinks it over for a few seconds. By the time he decides on the colors, Bubba and Pop-Pop are busy talking with Jake's therapists, so my only audience is Freddy, who's seen the trick a million times. I'm about to hand the crayons back to him when Peter rolls up next to us.

"Do you want to try?" I ask him.

He nods. As I put the crayons on his wheelchair tray, someone grabs me from behind and squeezes my ribs. It doesn't take a mind reader to guess who. "Katie, I'm trying to do a magic trick here."

"I love magic tricks!" She squeezes me even harder. I wonder if this sort of thing ever happens to Magnus.

Just then, Mom announces that the quiz has ended. She reads the questions out loud and people shout the answers—half of which are wrong. Tina gets the most right (I would have, but Mom wouldn't let me—or Freddy—play) and wins a gift card to a local bookstore. She goes straight to Jake, who's sitting in Mrs. Todd's lap, and gives him a kiss. "I know all about you," Tina says, "because I love you so much."

Next we all sing "Happy Birthday" and "For He's a Jolly Good Fellow" for Jake as Dad brings out the cake. Freddy helps Jake blow out two Tweety Bird candles, and Mandy tries to feed Jake a little spoonful of icing. He wrinkles his nose and makes a face.

"I don't think Jakey likes it," Freddy says.

Mom carries the rest of the cake to the kitchen counter to cut it up while Katie's mom and Tina scoop out different flavors of ice cream. Freddy and I are in charge of handing out the plates.

Katie's mom sighs. "This is a perfect party. I went to one last week that was a disaster."

Mom continues dividing the sheet cake as evenly as she can. "What happened?"

Katie's mom leans in close to mine. "Two kids couldn't play on any equipment because they were in wheelchairs."

"We need more playgrounds like the one at Sequoia,

where there's something for everyone," Mom says. "Like special swings and raised sandboxes—"

"So?" Freddy pipes up. "Why don't we get some?"

Katie's mom ruffles his hair. "I wish we could, sweetie. It's all very expensive."

"We should throw a fund-raiser," Tina says. "I bet I can get a bunch of people from school to help. We could hold a spaghetti dinner—"

Mom stops plating. "That's a terrific idea. I'm sure I can put together a bake sale." Mom loves putting together bake sales.

Tina grins. "And live music! Maybe my high school jazz band . . ."

I do love the jazz band. This actually might be fun.

Freddy turns to me. "And you can do magic tricks!" he says, his mouth full of cake.

"I guess . . . if people want me to." It would be pretty awesome to perform on the same stage as the high school band. It's nothing like Magic Fest, of course, but it would still be the biggest audience I've ever had. . . .

Besides, this is exactly the kind of thing Magnus would do. And that makes me want to do it even more.

CHAPTER EIGHTEEN

Every time our parents throw one of us a birthday party, they get all worn out, so the minute we're back home they retreat to take a nap. Jake's wide awake though, so I carry him to the big green sofa for another exciting round of Super Jake versus the King of Chaos! The wrestling match begins when I put all thirty pounds' worth of Jake on top of me, then try to get out from under him. Even though I put up a good fight, he wins every time. Wanna know his secret weapon?

Drool.

After that, Freddy and I dress Jake like a secret agent with sunglasses and one of Dad's old hats. Jake and I are about to bop the bad guy (Freddy, of course) with Elmo when a UPS truck pulls into our driveway.

I answer the door before the delivery person can even ring the bell.

The three of us shake the package and try to guess what's inside before we add it to the stack of unopened gifts from the party.

Freddy goes first. "Sounds like *Star Wars* toys!"

"I think it sounds like magic tricks," I joke. "What do you think, Jake?" I help him shake it. "He thinks it's a big mushy bowl of rice cereal."

Freddy giggles.

"What's going on?" Mom asks, coming into the room.

"Another present for Jake," I tell her. "It's from Uncle Steve."

"Can we open them now?" Freddy is practically clawing at the presents, he's so excited.

"No time like the present for presents," Dad says as he joins us.

Freddy and I pile all the gifts on the living room table and Mom gets a pen and paper to keep track for thank-you notes. Dad holds Jake in his arms and helps him open the first gift: a fuzzy brown teddy bear with a red sleeping cap—from Chris and his parents. Dad slides Jake's fingers along the soft fur.

The therapists all gave Jake gifts that are fun for Freddy and me, too: toys that light up, toys that play music—and one that does both. Freddy tries out each one while Dad and Jake open the rest of the presents.

Both sets of grandparents pitched in and bought Jake a swing that goes for fifteen minutes at a time, and Tina made Jake a Winnie the Pooh quilt. Uncle Steve sent presents for every one of us, because he's cool like that: an autographed book for Mom by one of her favorite authors; a funny T-shirt for Dad; a Jack-in-the-Box for Jake; a Yoda doll for Freddy; and a new Marvel DVD for me.

Uncle Steve is the best.

"One last gift," Mom says. She reaches for a huge box, and opens the card first. "It's from Wendy and Rox."

"Maybe it's a billion-piece *Star Wars* Lego!" Freddy shouts.

"It's for Jake, not you," I remind him.

Dad hands Mom a pair of scissors and we all watch as she cuts the tape and opens the flaps. Her smile disappears. "Diapers."

"Diapers?" Freddy repeats, like he can't believe it.

"Well ..." Dad says after a few seconds. "Who wants pizza?"

Most days, that's another one of those rhetorical questions Ms. Carlin likes. Freddy and I love pizza, any day, any time. Except this time.

"No, thanks," I say.

"I'm not hungry," Freddy says.

Freddy and I retreat to the other room to play video games, but we both just sit staring at the blank TV screen.

"Diapers are dumb," Freddy says. "What kind of birthday present is that?"

I shrug. "I guess Rox doesn't know what Jake likes."

"He likes lots of things!" Freddy counts on his fingers. "Lollipops, applesauce, whipped cream, Clifford the Big Red Dog, *Goodnight Moon* . . ."

"You're right."

Freddy gets quiet, so I know he's thinking really hard. "Diapers are dumb."

A few hours later, when I go to tell Jake good night, I can't believe what I see: Bugs Bunny on one side of his pillow and Freddy's brand-new Yoda doll on the other. I grab something from my room, then go to Freddy's. He's sitting in bed with one of his *Star Wars* books, Pita Rabbit at his side.

I hold out my hands with the fingers closed so he can't see what I'm hiding. "Wanna see what's inside?"

He nods and sits up a little straighter.

I open my hands and show him a bunch of crayons. "Pick one."

His eyes go wide. "Is this the trick you did at Jake's party?"

"Maybe."

His eyes go wider. "Are you going to teach it to me?"

"Maybe."

He jumps off the bed and hugs me.

"Okay, okay." I turn my back to him. "First, you've got to choose a color."

He takes a year and a half to decide, but for once I don't mind.

"Ready!"

He puts the crayon in my right hand, then I turn around and face him, bringing my left hand up front and "concentrating" really hard.

"Hmmm. I'm seeing fire engines and strawberries and cherry lollipops. Is it red?"

"How did you guess?" he asks, mystified.

"You have to promise not to show anyone else, okay?"

"I promise!"

So I show him how it works. (Ethan's Rule #5: Like everyone knows, there's an exception to every rule. Here's mine: when someone does something really nice for someone else, they deserve to learn an awesome magic trick.)

He tries it. Over and over again. It takes a while, but he doesn't give up. And when he finally gets it right, his smile is almost bigger than his entire face.

And it makes me smile, too.

CHAPTER NINETEEN

Winter break is finally happening.

Magic Fest is not.

Between Jake's party being a hit, and getting into the holiday spirit, I was hoping Dad would change his mind . . . but he hasn't.

Today Freddy's going to Tyler's house, and Jake's got a playdate with Wendy at her house, so Mom and I decide to visit our favorite diner again.

As usual, our pink-haired waitress greets us with a big smile. "Ethan, I'll give you a quarter if you order something instead of grilled cheese," she teases.

If I were still trying to get money for Magic Fest, I'd be tempted to take her up on it. "Maybe next time."

"A girl can dream, right?" She laughs and walks away to place our usual order.

Mom and I are halfway through our food when her cell rings.

"Hey, Rox, is everything . . . what?"

I put down what's left of my sandwich and wait to see if we're about to race over to Rox's house. Wait to hear if Jake is okay.

A few seconds go by, then Mom's shoulders relax and I know Jake's all right.

"No, that's fine. He's fine. He probably just . . . he might not be hungry yet. Really. It's okay." Mom looks at me, smiles, and shakes her head. "We'll see you in a little bit." She ends the call. "Jake doesn't want his lunch."

"Maybe he's holding out for grilled cheese."

She laughs. "Maybe so."

"Do you want to skip dessert?" I ask, hoping she'll say no.

"How 'bout we get something to go and share it with Rox? Sounds like she could use it."

Great. Maybe Ned can join us and we can all sit around the table together. Fun times.

The thought of even possibly seeing Ned makes me lose my appetite.

Mom orders a slice of six-layer cake that's big enough for a family of ten.

"Try not to eat it all in one sitting." Our waitress smiles, then leaves to grab our check and take-out box.

Mom shakes her head again, only this time she's not smiling. "She means well."

"The waitress?"

"Rox."

I'm not sure what to say.

"She just doesn't know how to act around Jake."

"Then she should ask."

"She should. But maybe she thinks it's kinder not to ask at all."

"Why?"

Mom takes a last sip of her coffee. "Maybe she thinks it's hard for us to talk about Jake."

I think about that as Mom puts money on the table for the tip. "If Rox doesn't ask, maybe you should just tell her."

Mom smiles and reaches for my hand. "How did you get to be so smart?"

———————

"I'm so sorry I ruined your lunch," Rox says for the third time as she slices the cake.

"You didn't ruin anything," Mom answers for the third time. It's like a really boring Ping-Pong game. "Jake just has to get used to you, like we had to get used to him." She stops feeding Jake. "Would you like to try again? I bet he'll let you feed him this time."

"Sure." Rox looks at Jake. "If you think it's okay."

Mom hands the jar and spoon to her and they switch seats. Rox dips the spoon into the jar and offers it to Jake. Sure enough, Jake gobbles it up. Rox looks a thousand times happier. I watch Jake and Rox make their way through the rest of the peaches together while Mom pours apple juice into a bottle, then adds white powdery stuff to it, stirring it in.

"What's that?" Rox asks.

"We add thickener to his liquids so he won't drink too fast and choke," Mom explains.

"I've never seen that before," Rox says.

"It's no big deal." As Mom shakes the bottle, she looks over at me, then back at Rox. "You should have seen Jake when we first brought him home."

I'm glad she's finally going to tell Rox all about Jake; I just don't want to hear it. I move my fork around, moving all the crumbs into a pile. Mom looks at me again, reading my mind as usual.

"Ethan? Want to go see if Wendy's still napping?"

"I guess."

"She's right down the hall," Rox says.

It's easy enough to find Wendy's room: it's got a lavender door and a purple sequined tiara stuck to it.

I crack the door and peek inside; she's fast asleep under a

Hello Kitty comforter, sucking her thumb. I close her door and head back down the hall when I hear something, no, someone. Someone who is crying.

It has to be Ned.

I stop outside what I assume is his bedroom door, a billion thoughts and feelings swirling around, all jumbled up in my head.

Part of me doesn't care if he's sad and hurting. But another part of me feels sorry for him with his dad being so far away. Even when my dad and I are upset with each other, like now, I know he's still here for me.

Ned's stopped crying. I should probably go back to Mom and Rox. I should *definitely* go back. . . .

My hand knocks on his door. I hear the scrape of a chair being pulled across the floor and footsteps heading my way. I could still run . . . but I don't.

The door opens. Ned's eyes are red and wide open in surprise. "What are *you* doing here?"

I say the first thing that pops into my head: "There's cake."

He stares at me like I'm insane.

"It's really good."

Still staring.

"Do you like cake?"

"Is something wrong with you?"

"Plenty," I tell him. "But cake helps . . ."

He snorts. "Cake can't help me."

I shrug. "Can't hurt to try."

He stares at me a little longer, then tilts his head the way Freddy does. "What flavor is it?"

CHAPTER TWENTY

Today's the last day of winter break, so I'm going to make it a good one.

It definitely starts that way. Mom makes Freddy's and my favorite breakfast: chocolate waffles.

After breakfast, Freddy and I have a "therapy session" with Jake. Only we make it fun.

Freddy and I take the teddy bear Jake got for his birthday and turn it into a terrifying Ninja Bear by changing his sleeping cap into a red hood that covers his face.

I help Jake track the ruthless villain from right to left and up and down, then we work on arm stretching by punching Ninja Bear and hurling him across the room. Freddy runs and fetches the stuffed animal like a puppy, and we do it again and again until Wendy shows up for another playdate.

While Rox and Mom help Wendy out of her purple coat,

purple mittens, and purple boots, I head outside before Mom makes me put on so many layers of clothing that I can't move. And I need to move fast! It's been snowing like crazy the past two days, and it's the perfect kind of snow . . . for a snowball fight.

My friends come over and we divide into teams. The four of us spend the first few minutes building an arsenal of snowballs, then head for my backyard. Daniel and I lob snowballs from behind a gigantic oak tree, and our opponents grab trash cans and use them for cover. There are so many snowballs flying around it's impossible to tell which side wins, but we're having too much fun to care.

When our fingers and faces are numb, Mom gives us mugs of steaming hot soup, then Daniel and Brian head home. After that, it's time for *Super Smash Bros.* and *Mario Kart*. Then the two of us have a fencing match with Jake's bubble wands, which work surprisingly well. The biggest surprise of all, though, is how much fun I had all day . . . with Ned.

Since it *is* the last day of winter break, when Dad gets home from running errands all day, he makes a fire in the fireplace and the five of us gather in front of it. Mom holds Jake, Freddy holds a bag of marshmallows, and I toast one at a time 'til they're perfect: golden brown on the outside, and gooey on the inside.

"How was Jake's playdate?" Dad asks as he turns over a log.

Mom smiles. "He and Wendy played grocery store and looked at her favorite picture books. Then she colored a picture of Snow White for him and made him a puppy out of Play-Doh." She strokes Jake's chubby cheek. "You had a wonderful time, didn't you?"

"Ethan had a nice playdate, too," Freddy says.

Dad stirs the fire some more. "Oh? Did Daniel and Brian come over?"

"Yep." I pass a marshmallow to Freddy, who has his hand out for the third time.

"But Ned stayed the longest." Freddy bites into the marshmallow and sticky white goo explodes on his face.

Dad stops playing with the fire and turns his attention on me. "You spent the day with Ned?"

I shrug. "We pretty much spent it fighting."

Mom laughs. "With snowballs and bubble wands."

Dad looks at me, then at Mom. She nods, even though he didn't ask her anything. They do that a lot. I never know what they're talking about, so I take a marshmallow from Freddy, spear it, and hold it over the fire.

I guess all the snowball fights and video games with Ned wore me out. I wake up on top of my blanket with *Prisoner of Azkaban* by my side and a knock at my door.

"Can I come in?" Dad asks.

"Sure."

He takes a seat on my bed. "I'm proud of you, E. I don't know when, or how, but you managed to turn someone you fought with into someone you're friends with."

"I didn't really do anything. It just kind of happened."

"Well . . ." Dad reaches inside his shirt pocket. "This just kind of happened, too."

And he hands me the registration ticket to Magic Fest.

CHAPTER TWENTY-ONE

Ever since I got my Magic Fest registration ticket back, I've been trying really hard to prepare for the competition. It's less than a week away now, which would be great—if I hadn't lost so much time. Some days, I feel like my act is almost there; some days, I think it'll never be good enough.

Mom and Dad seem to understand and are giving me some slack so I can catch up. Every chance I get, I'm working on my King of Chaos routine. And when I'm not working on it, I'm going over it in my head, wondering if there's a better, or funnier, way to perform each trick.

This is not helping my grades.

Luckily, I've got that report on heroes coming up in English, which counts for 40 percent of our grade, and I know I'm gonna ace it.

There's tons of reasons I look up to Magnus: The way he

walks into a room and instantly has everyone's attention. The way he does every single trick perfectly, every single time, and makes it look so easy. And how, whenever someone interviews him, he says the exact right thing and never loses his cool, no matter how dumb the question is. I bet he could even handle Miss Wright's class.

What makes him a hero to me, though, are the things he does that really matter, like this thing he did called "Live below the Line," to raise awareness of hunger and poverty. He lived on a dollar and fifty cents' worth of food every day for a week, which is basically a cup of rice and a baked potato. What makes Magnus heroic is that he uses his fame to help people— to make a difference.

If I ever become a famous magician, I'm gonna do that, too (except for the rice and baked potato).

It's finally the weekend, and that means I have more time than usual to work on my King of Chaos routine. Since juggling is one of the weakest parts of the act, I decide to juggle everything in sight (except for knives). It's going pretty well until I grab some eggs off the counter.

I really thought they were hard-boiled.

"Sorry," I tell Mom as she hands me a wet paper towel. I wipe the yucky egg mess off the floor. "I feel like if I don't practice every second I can, I'll never be ready for Magic Fest."

She takes the goopy paper towel and hands me a dry one. "Ethan, your act is terrific. You're more than ready. There's only one thing you need."

"A rabbit?"

Mom laughs. "Confidence." She pulls me in for a hug. "How would you like to do a practice show for a small but friendly audience?"

"That would be amazing."

"How about tomorrow afternoon?"

"Tomorrow?"

"It just so happens I've invited some people over for that very reason." She smiles.

"Who's coming?"

"You'll find out soon enough."

● ● ● ● ● ● ● ● ● ● ● ● ● ● ● ● ● ● ●

I tie on the purple velvet cape Tina made for me and, for the finishing touch, place a gold crown from an old costume on my head: the King of Chaos is in the house!

Dad gives a thumbs-up as he begins to record my performance, and Mom grins and holds Jake in her lap. My grandparents are there, too, along with Daniel and Brian, and Tina and the Todds. Wendy's waving. Rox is smiling. And Ned is, too.

I nod at Freddy, who's looking at me like I'm as magnificent as Magnus. He turns on the music and it's time for the King of Chaos world premiere!

After the main act—which goes flawlessly—I do a few card tricks with audience participation and, just for fun, I even let Freddy do the crayon trick. I've never seen him happier.

I've never been happier, either.

I wonder if Magnus feels this way every time he performs—like life doesn't get better than this.

Like anything is possible.

———————————

After the show everybody stays a while talking and laughing and congratulating me. Then Dad and Freddy go out to a movie, Mom takes Jake to the park, and everyone else heads home for dinner—except Ned. We make ourselves sandwiches and popcorn and watch some TV, then he asks to see more card tricks.

We're in the middle of a lightsaber duel when Mom comes in carrying Jake and biting her lip.

"His temperature's high."

I keep fighting. I really don't want this to turn into a big deal in front of Ned. "Maybe he's teething again?" I suggest.

She shakes her head. "I don't think so. I have to get him in the tub and cool him down."

"Okay..."

"I need your help."

"Can't it wait a few more minutes? Ned and I are—"

"LISTEN TO ME. I have to get Jake in the tub and I need you to call Dr. Albert for me. NOW." When Mom talks in capital letters, there's no use arguing. She heads to the bathroom and I hear the water turning on.

"Sorry," I tell Ned.

I hit number two on the speed dial.

"What's going on?" he asks.

"When Jake's temperature gets too high—" A nurse answers before I can finish explaining. "Hi, um, this is Ethan Miller. Jake's big brother? My mom—" Before I say another word, she puts me on hold to connect me to Dr. Albert.

Next thing I know, Mom's on the phone and I'm sponging Jake down in his bath chair while stupid Big Bird smiles on the washcloth.

I hate Big Bird.

Ned stands at the bathroom door, watching. "What's that?" He points at Jake's bath chair.

"Jake can't sit up by himself, and it's hard to hold him and wash him at the same time. So we strap him in with this special seat."

I squeeze Jake's pudgy wet hands together. Even though his cheeks are flushed and he looks tired, he still finds a smile for me.

"He likes that!" Ned takes a step closer.

"Ethan?" Mom calls from down the hall.

I look at Ned. "Would you mind watching him for a sec?"

Panic sweeps across his face and I almost laugh. Ned the Giant is scared of a two-year-old. "What do I do?"

"Just keep him company," I tell him on my way out.

When I get to Mom, she asks me to get Jake out of the tub and bring him to her.

I head back down the hall, afraid to see what's going on. What if Ned says something mean about Jake again? I don't know if I could forgive him this time. We're friends now, and he should know better. Shouldn't he?

I crack the door open and can't believe what I see: Ned's singing "Splish Splash" and squeezing a rubber duckie between Jake's hands.

All I can do is stand and stare. After a few seconds, Ned notices me. "I think he's feeling better." He squeezes Jake's hands just like I did a few minutes earlier.

I kneel next to the tub and take a good look at Jake. It's true—he's definitely looking more like himself. I lift Jake out of the tub and splash a little powder on him the way Mom taught me.

"Hey, Ethan?" Ned says softly as I wrap Jake in a fluffy blue towel. "I'm really sorry. About calling Jake . . . you know."

I look over at him. He really does look like he's sorry. "It's okay." I want to leave it at that, but I can't. "I'm sorry, too. About shoving you and everything."

Ned shrugs. "I deserved it. Besides, it's not like it hurt. I'm pretty tough." He squeaks the rubber duckie and smiles at my little brother.

I have to smile, too. *He's pretty tough all right.*

By the time Dad and Freddy are back, so is Jake's appetite. When Ned leaves, he invites me to try a new video game at his house next weekend. And he says I should bring Jake along. For Wendy.

I'm in my room working on my one-handed shuffle when Mom calls, "Ethan! Freddy! You've got to see this!"

Freddy and I both rush out of our rooms and sprint to the living room.

"Look! I found a new way to make Jake smile." Mom's in front of the Kid Kart, brushing bright pink crinkly paper on Jake's cheeks. He always smiles when you squish it in his hands or in front of his face. But *on* the face is something new and Jake's not just smiling; he's seconds away from laughing— something he's never done before!

One of these days he will, and I'll laugh right along with him, louder than anyone.

CHAPTER TWENTY-TWO

"Ethan, wake up! We have to go."

The glowing green numbers on my bedside clock show 3:10 a.m.

The hallway light is on, and I can make out just enough of Mom's face to see she looks scared. So scared I get a sick feeling deep inside.

"What's wrong?" I jump out of bed and race toward my closet to grab some clothes.

"There's no time," Mom says, her voice tight and strained, like even words are dangerous. "Jake's not doing well."

My heart's doing double time as I follow her into Jake's room. Then it just about stops. Jake's blue eyes are wide open and his face is so flushed it looks sunburned. His tiny chest is heaving, like he doesn't remember how to breathe. It's hard for me to breathe, too; I've never seen him like this.

Dad's on the bed, wiping Jake's forehead and cheeks with a wet towel. Mom's racing around tossing things into the Pooh bag. I feel Freddy pressing up behind me, but I'm afraid to look away from Jake even for a second.

"Is Jakey going to be all right?" Freddy asks, sounding as frightened as I feel.

No one answers his question. All Mom says is, "Let's go."

We throw our coats over our pajamas, Mom grabs Jake, Dad grabs the Pooh bag, and I grab Freddy. What seems like seconds later, we're screeching out of the driveway.

The sky is black. Our car is the only one on the road. Dad's driving so fast, I'm sure he's breaking the speed limit.

I close my eyes, hoping this is a dream and that I'll wake up any second. When I open them, Jake's still in his car seat between Freddy and me, his breaths coming hard and fast.

I want to tell him he'll feel better soon. But the words don't come. All I can do is hold on to his hot, tiny hand as the minivan speeds through the darkness closing in all around us.

The Emergency Room nurse takes one look at Jake as we rush over to the front desk and says, "Come with me." She hurries down a long white hall, Mom close behind, Jake held tightly in her arms. Freddy and I start after her, but Dad holds us back. We watch Mom, Jake, and the nurse disappear around a corner. Big metal doors slam shut behind them.

"Why can't we go, too?" Freddy asks.

"Mom will take care of him. Don't worry. Jake's gonna be okay," I tell him.

Then I look at Dad. "Right?"

Dad glances my way and opens his mouth. He looks me in the eye for what feels like forever. And finally he says, "I don't know."

As scary as the past hour has already been, that scares me more than anything.

———————

The big black hands on the waiting room clock show we've been sitting in this crummy place half an hour. We're still waiting to see Jake.

I stretch my arms and legs, rotate my head in one direction and then the other. Then I start cracking my knuckles. It's not like there's much else to do.

"Hey, Ethan, wanna play tic-tac-toe?" Freddy asks.

"No."

Only Freddy would want to play a game at a time like this. He shoves a piece of paper in my face and hands me a pen with the hospital's name printed on it.

My hand draws a big fat *X* in the top left corner of the tic-tac-toe grid.

Fifteen minutes and a thousand tic-tac-toe games later, Freddy tugs on Dad's sleeve. "I'm hungry."

Dad fishes around in his pocket for some change and hands it to Freddy, who races over to the vending machine. "Ethan, do you want anything?"

I shake my head no. All I want is to know how Jake is.

———————————

It's four-thirty in the morning. Freddy's lips are stained neon orange from his cheesy snack, and his eyes are closed. I don't know how he can sleep in these uncomfortable chairs.

I don't know how he can sleep at all.

Dad squeezes my shoulder. "You can nap, too, if you're tired. I'll wake you as soon as there's any news."

There's no way I'm sleeping 'til I know Jake's all right.

I stand up to show Dad that I'm the opposite of tired. I want to go for a walk, only I don't want to go too far. I want to go for a run, only I don't know where to run to.

So I pace from one end of the dingy waiting room to the other. I pace back and forth until my legs and feet are as tired as the rest of me.

Then I do it some more.

———————————

"Daddy, will you read me this story?"

Freddy's wide awake again. He brings over some picture book he found somewhere.

Dad clears his throat, wraps an arm around Freddy, and starts to read in a quiet bedtime voice, even though we're the only ones here. He stops after a few sentences and asks if I'd like to look at one of the magazines on the table next to him.

NO! I don't want to look at a stupid magazine! But what I say is, "No, thanks. I'm okay."

I stare at the clock, wishing the hands would move faster and we'd all be home again. Wishing the hands would go backward and everything would be all right again. Watching the second hand make its way around the circle, over and over and over . . .

———————————

My eyes are burning. My brain is screaming. Dad's gone beyond the big metal doors a couple times. When he comes back, all he says is they're still helping Jake.

I try to think about something else. About Magic Fest and magic tricks and "Abracadabra" and . . .

Abracadabra, abracadabra, abracadabracadabracadab

I remember this game Mom and I used to play, where we'd take a big word and see how many small words we could make out of it. I do it now, in my head. Abracadabra: card, crab, car, bar, bad.

Bad. How bad? Really bad?

Bad badbadbadbadbadbadbadbad . . .

Why can't we see Jake? Just for a minute? Just for a second! Why isn't anyone telling us anything? And where the heck is—

"Mommy!" Freddy jumps up and runs to her.

I jump up, too, then I notice how dazed she looks, how pale her face is. She looks more like a robot than my mother.

Dad stands up, his face one gigantic question mark. Part of me wants to ask how Jake is doing and when we can see him; part of me isn't sure I want to know.

"Is Jakey okay?" Freddy blurts out.

"His temperature was very high," Mom says in a quiet, shaky voice. "It's lower now, but we don't know if . . . we're not sure how . . ." She stops talking, like she's run out of energy or words. She looks at Dad and he takes over.

"The doctors and nurses are doing everything they can to help Jake," Dad says. He puts his arms around Mom, and Freddy wraps himself around her legs.

I can't move. I think I'm gonna throw up.

Mom leans against Dad for so long, I'm starting to think they've forgotten all about me. Then Mom wipes her eyes, looks at me, and announces, "Emma and Bubba are on their way."

"Why?"

"They'll stay with you until we're back home."

"Wait. You're staying here?"

Mom keeps talking, like she's reciting a speech she's memorized. "If we're not home after school—"

"I'm not going to school! I'm not leaving until I know Jake's okay!" I shout, maybe a little too loudly for a waiting room.

"Me neither!" Freddy says.

"Ethan, Freddy," Dad says in his extra-calm, don't-mess-with-me voice, "you two are going home. There's nothing you can do for Jake right now. You need to get some sleep, maybe go to school."

"But . . ."

Mom gives Freddy and me quick hugs and a kiss, then turns and does her robot walk toward the big metal doors. They open electronically and she disappears.

Somewhere behind those doors, Jake is trying to breathe.

He's gotta be scared. If I could just squeeze his hands, I'm sure he'd feel better, knowing I'm there.

"Dad, can't I please, *please* stay?" He shakes his head, but I don't give him a chance to say no. "Emma and Bubba can take Freddy and—"

"Ethan, don't make this harder than it already is."

There's something in Dad's voice I've never heard before.

And then I realize: he's every bit as scared as I am.

And all the fight goes out of me.

When Emma and Bubba show up, Freddy and I leave without another word. There's nothing left to say. Jake is staying. Mom and Dad are staying.

I'm not.

My stomach is killing me. My legs weigh a thousand pounds. Bubba puts an arm around me and leads me out the door and into the car. It's all I can do not to jump out and run back into the hospital. Run back and find Jake.

Leaving him behind is the hardest thing I've ever done.

CHAPTER TWENTY-THREE

It's not Emma's fault, but after the early morning ER visit, she makes the worst breakfast ever. Even my favorite cereal doesn't taste right.

Bubba smiles too hard. "I know what you need." He brings Freddy and me steaming mugs of cocoa and a bag of marshmallows. Freddy dumps in some mini marshmallows, then stares into space. I take a sip and burn my tongue.

Emma reaches across the table and puts her hand on mine. "If you want to stay home today from school it will be all right. I can write a note to your teachers."

I consider it for a minute. Only I know my staying home isn't gonna help Jake. And if I go to school, at least I'll see my friends and be busy and maybe not think about how scary things are with Jake.

"It's okay. I'll go. I don't want to get behind in my classes."

Yeah, right.

"Can I stay home?" Freddy asks. "I can watch *SpongeBob* and work on the jigsaw puzzle!"

Emma smiles and shakes her head. "You can do that *after* school."

As bad as school is on a regular Monday, it's even worse when I don't know how Jake is. When the last bell finally rings, I race out of the building. He's probably home by now.

I'm so anxious to get there, I almost miss Chris standing at my corner next to Betty the Crossing Guard.

"Hey, Ethan." Chris is smiling, but it looks a little phony. Something is wrong.

"Hey."

"Guess what? We're going to hang out at my house this afternoon. I talked my mom into making those mint brownies you like."

"Okay . . ."

He starts walking toward home and I follow.

"Is Jake still at the hospital?" I ask.

"Actually," Chris says, "he's at a different hospital now— your parents are with him. Your grandparents, too."

"Why? What's wrong with the hospital he was at? He always goes there. It's close to home, and the doctors always take good care of him."

"I'm sure they do," Chris says. "But this new hospital? The doctors there *only* take care of children."

"Is that good or bad?"

Chris stops walking and turns to face me. "I don't know. I mean, I guess it's good because that's what they specialize in, so . . . they should be able to help Jake."

"But is he doing better or worse?"

He lets out a deep breath. "My mom told me Jake's temperature spiked while you and Freddy were at school." He waits for me to say something, or maybe to ask more questions. But I don't know what to say or ask. I don't know what to think.

"Try not to worry," Chris says. "I'm sure your parents will call as soon as they know more."

Kids walk by, laughing about something, but it feels awfully quiet where we're standing.

"Hey. I cleaned up the bunk beds for you guys . . . in case your parents don't come home until late and you sleep over."

Any other day, spending the night at Chris's would be great. Freddy and I have been pestering him to try out those bunk beds forever. All I do now is shrug.

We go to his house and I drop my backpack and trumpet off, then Chris and I walk down the hill toward Freddy's bus stop. When his bus pulls up, Freddy runs over to us—he's all smiles, excited to see Chris. Then he looks at me and knows something is up. "What's wrong?"

"Nothing," I tell him. He looks at me, unconvinced. I sigh. "Mom and Dad are still with Jake at the hospital."

His eyes get huge. "Still?"

"They'll be home soon," I say, hoping it's true.

"In the meantime, you guys are coming to my house," Chris says. "Okay?"

Freddy looks at me again, and I know I have to act like everything's fine so he's not scared. "Guess what? Tonight we finally get to try Chris's bunk beds!"

"All right!" Freddy smiles and Chris nods at me as if to say, "Good job." I'm glad Freddy is excited. Wish I was.

When we get back to Chris's house, Mrs. Todd offers us a snack but I'm not hungry, so I go to the living room to get my math homework over with.

I get stuck on the first problem. "I hate math," I mumble.

"Need some help?" Chris looks up from the book he's reading.

I didn't realize I'd said that out loud.

"Let's see." Chris studies the example. "I think I remember how to do this. . . ." He takes a piece of paper and finishes the problem in two seconds. We get the whole thing done in fifteen minutes, then I find Freddy in the sunroom, erasing something on his worksheet. "I hate math," he says.

"Need some help?" I ask.

He nods and we get to work. Lucky for him, I can still do first-grade math.

"Hey, Ethan," he looks up with a hopeful smile, "you think someday I'll help Jake with his math homework?"

"I don't know. How much is eight plus two?"

He counts on his fingers. "Twelve?"

—————————

After our homework is done, Mrs. Todd joins us for the most exciting card game ever: Go Fish. We're on the hundredth game when the phone finally rings. Mrs. Todd answers right away. "Ethan? It's your—"

I race over and grab the phone. "Hello?"

"How are you, sweetie?" Mom asks.

"I'm fine. How's Jake?" I wait for her to say something, but there's this long pause that makes me really nervous. "How is Jake?" I ask again.

"The doctors are still running tests." Her voice doesn't sound right.

"He's okay, though, right?"

"Ethan, they're calling Daddy and me. I'll talk to you soon."

"Wait! When are you coming home?"

"Sweetie, I've got to go. I love you."

Before I can even say "I love you" back, I hear the phone click off.

Everyone is looking at me, but no one says a thing. I guess no one knows what to say. Finally, Mrs. Todd clears her throat. "Since you two are spending the night, would you like to go home and get some things? Pajamas? Toothbrushes?"

"I guess," I say.

"I guess," Freddy echoes.

We trudge across the street and I let us into the house with my spare key.

"Need any help packing?" I ask Freddy.

He shakes his head, so I go to my room and pull out the suitcase I thought I'd be packing for Magic Fest this Thursday night. I toss in clothes, juggling balls, and the fourth Harry Potter book. Then I go to Jake's room, look around for a second or two, and grab something that makes me feel like Jake is with me.

I'm putting the item in my suitcase when Freddy shows up at my door. "Ready," he says. Then he notices Tweety in my hands and I feel like I've been caught doing something I shouldn't.

"I'm glad you're bringing Tweety." He reaches into his *Star Wars* backpack and pulls out Pita Rabbit. "They can hang out together."

We get through dinner and watch TV with Chris and his parents, but it's no fun, really. When it's time for bed, I think Freddy and I are both glad to go to the guest room where the bunk beds are.

"Want the top bunk?" I ask Freddy.

"That's okay," he says. "I'll take the bottom."

"How 'bout we take turns? I get it tonight; you get it tomorrow?" One look at his face tells me I screwed up. Neither of us wants to be here tomorrow night. "I mean, if we're still here. Which we probably won't be."

He takes out his Spidey doll, Han Solo action figure, and Pita Rabbit and squishes them next to him on the bottom bunk.

"Want Tweety down there, too?"

"That's okay. You can keep him."

I turn out the light, leaving the door open a crack so we can find our way in the dark if we need to.

"Wanna come up for a while? It's pretty fun being so high up." My voice sounds fake even to my own ears.

He doesn't answer.

"Okay," I say, giving it my best shot. "It's crunchy, orange, and grows in the ground. . . ."

"A carrot," Freddy says in the dark.

"Good job!" When all else fails, play the food game. "Your turn."

It's quiet for so long I wonder if he's fallen asleep. "Okay," he finally says. "It's all different colors, and it's really yummy. And sticky. And messy, but not at first."

"Icing?"

"Nope."

"A bar of soap?"

"No." Freddy giggles. "Want another hint?"

"Sure."

"Jake likes it."

I see a bright pink tongue and even brighter smile. "Cotton candy," I whisper.

CHAPTER TWENTY-FOUR

I basically sleepwalk to school but manage to stay awake through most of my classes. When I get home, our minivan is in the carport and Mom is at the front door. I race up the driveway and she squeezes me in a bear hug.

"I can't breathe!" I gasp.

She squeezes even harder, then stares at me like she's been away for years.

"How's Jake? When can I see him? Is he coming home soon?"

"He's better and you can see him later this week. As far as coming home soon, I sure hope so." She strokes my hair like when I was little.

The timer rings and I follow her into the kitchen. She pulls two pans of warm chocolate cupcakes out of the oven: one of my favorite things on the planet.

"Why don't you start your homework while these cool?

Then we'll ice them together, and you can help me figure out what to take to Jake tomorrow."

"His jingle sticks for sure. And crinkly paper. Red, maybe. Or green. And you *gotta* bring a Beatles CD! And Tweety Bird, and *Goodnight Moon*. Maybe you can bring Jake a cupcake!"

Mom smiles back at me. "Maybe so."

As great as the cupcakes are, having Mom and Dad home is even better. The three of us play some board games with Freddy, and I read aloud from *Merlin*—two chapters instead of one, since we've missed so many lately.

After Freddy goes to sleep, Mom and I talk for a while about Jake . . . but only about happy things, like his first bottle and his birthday party and his playdates with Wendy. Once or twice I almost mention Magic Fest, since it's only three days from now. But it doesn't feel like the right time—or even the right thing to talk about. For tonight, I'm just happy to have both of my parents home again, and to know Jake will be home soon, too.

● ● ● ● ● ● ● ● ● ● ● ● ● ● ● ● ● ●

It feels like things are almost back to normal—until I see Chris the next day, waiting for me after school. My feet stop moving. My heart practically stops, too.

"Don't worry," he says. "Everyone is fine. Your parents will be home for supper, and Freddy's with your grandparents."

My heart rate goes back to normal and I let out a breath.

He starts walking, so I do, too. "I was wondering if you had time to go bowling?"

I stop dead in my tracks. "Bowling?"

He turns with a smile. "Unless you're anxious to get to your math homework?"

A few minutes later we're in his car, riding with the windows down and the radio up.

"Chris? How come three strikes in baseball is bad, but three strikes in bowling is good?"

He laughs. "That's a great question."

He doesn't have a great answer, but I don't care. And I don't care that I don't get any strikes, either. It's fun just hanging out. After the first game, we buy a pitcher of lemonade and watch the other bowlers. I'm wondering if I'll get any strikes the next game when Chris says, "Listen . . ."

The serious expression on his face makes my stomach hurt. I don't know what's coming, but I know it's gonna be bad. I lean forward and sit on the edge of the plastic chair, my right leg bouncing up and down.

"Even though Jake's doing a lot better, your parents don't feel right leaving him."

"I'm not going to Magic Fest, am I?" I sink into the chair like I have no bones.

I've been working so hard and waiting so long and wanting this so much. . . .

"So your parents and I were wondering if I could take you," Chris says. "That is, if it's okay with you."

"What?" I sit up straight. I picture the two of us, talking in the car, hanging out in the hotel room, watching magic acts together. I lean toward him. "Jake really is doing better, right?"

"Scout's honor." Chris does that thing with his fingers scouts do. Which, since he went all the way to Eagle Scout, he should know.

And just like that, everything is okay—better than okay. Chris and I are going to Magic Fest in two days!

• • • • • • • • • • • • • • • • •

The next day and a half go by crazy fast and suddenly—finally—I'm headed to Atlantic City. I'm so wired that Chris asks how many gallons of coffee I had for breakfast.

We have a great time on the ride up, talking and laughing and listening to music. Chris is a huge Beatles fan, and my parents are, too, so he puts a ton of Beatles songs on shuffle, and we play a game to see how fast we can name the song as soon as it begins. By the end, we're calling out names of songs before they even start. It's really fun. By the time we get to the hotel, my face hurts from smiling so much. Then we step into the lobby, and I know this will be the best time I've ever had, and the coolest thing I've ever done.

Everywhere I look, there are magicians: men, women, kids. In costumes, tuxedos and gowns, and casual clothes, like me. Some are working solo, others in pairs, doing card tricks, coin tricks, juggling, even mind-reading. There's so much excitement buzzing all around, I don't know what to do or where to go first.

While Chris checks us in, I try to soak up everything. The energy is electric and like nothing I've ever experienced. I wish I could put all the bright colors and happy chatter in a bottle and bring it home and pour it over my brothers—especially Jake. Instead, I do the next best thing: reach inside my jeans pocket for the red crinkly paper I brought along, and it's almost like Jake is here, too.

"We're all set." Chris flashes two keycards. "And there's plenty of time to look around some more before anything major starts."

By "anything major" he means the three contests. Everyone in my age category is in the first two contests: close-up and stage act. The stage acts start tomorrow morning, but the close-ups are today. Mine's at 4:15. The close-ups and stage act are both scored on a scale of one to ten by three judges. The categories are Showmanship, Technique/Skill, Originality, and Overall Entertainment Value.

The magicians with the top five scores win a hundred dollars and get to perform tomorrow night, in front of a huge audience, for the grand prize. This year there are forty-three junior magicians—and every single one of us came to win. For the first time since we arrived, it all feels real, instead of surreal . . . and the stakes are the most real of all.

The first thing Chris and I do is check out "The Dealer's Room," a gigantic ballroom filled with tricks and gadgets for sale.

"You look like Freddy at a toy store." Chris laughs.

We walk around for over an hour, checking out the latest and greatest magic tricks. Unfortunately, the best ones are really expensive. My favorite is "The Wizard's Ring." It looks like a regular ring, but there's a magnet inside. It can stop time on a watch, move forks and spoons, and make coins vanish.

Another one I like is "The Secret Tool of Crooked Gamblers," a card punch that marks cards so you can feel it, but not see it. Then there's "The Memorized Deck for the Forgetful," and shiny wooden wands. Maybe it's a good thing I don't have much extra money, because I wouldn't have it for very long in this shop!

After that, we decide to check out some of my competition. Since the close-ups are *close up*, there aren't many seats and three are for the judges.

It's fun watching the other junior magicians, but my mouth goes dry and my stomach feels tight. Am I good enough? I'm especially worried about Amazing Amelia. She's doing a funny act, too, and from what I could see, her close-up went perfectly.

I congratulate her afterward, even though she is a rival. A few minutes later, it's my turn. The judges take their seats, along with Chris and a dozen other people, including Amazing Amelia. That makes me even more nervous.

Luckily, I've practiced so much that even when I'm nervous, my hands know what to do. I open with a variation of the mini-marshmallows-into-big-marshmallow bit from my King of Chaos act, using candy kisses instead of marshmallows. I start with three silver cups and one candy kiss. As I shuffle them around, one kiss becomes two, and two become three. Then I shuffle the cups around until the kisses are gone, and a miniature candy bar appears instead.

The audience seems to enjoy it, especially when I reach into my top hat and shower them with candy kisses.

While they nibble their chocolate, I invite one of the judges to come up and pick a card. He shows it to the others and hands it back to me. I do the one-handed shuffle Jake helped me with and am about to find the card when I notice Chris texting on his cell phone in the middle of my routine.

I look at him like I can't believe it. "Really? You can't wait 'til my act is over?" I shout. I get up from behind my table and make a beeline for him as the stunned audience watches. I wait for him to put the phone away, which he does, looking slightly embarrassed.

I go back to my table, apologize to my audience, and pick the judge's card out of the deck. Only it's not the right one.

"Are you sure?" I ask.

The judge shakes his head. Amazing Amelia bites her lip, reminding me of my mom.

"Uh, can I try one more time?"

The judge nods. I pull out a different card, but it's still the wrong one. Now my audience is getting restless; people are shaking their heads, checking watches, fidgeting in their seats.

"It worked at home every time. Honest!" I shrug and sigh. "I don't know what happened to your card, Sir. I'm really sorry."

"Is this it?"

Everyone turns to look at Chris who, sure enough, is holding the right card.

When the judges smile and the audience applauds? It's magic.

———

To thank Chris for being my secret assistant, I treat him to an all-you-can-eat Chinese buffet. (And, believe me, he can eat. A lot.) While he chows down on chow mein, I play with my spring roll, unable to take even one bite.

"Ethan, relax! Your close-up routine was great. The judges loved you."

I let out a really long breath. "I hope so. I won't know for sure 'til the scores are up tomorrow morning."

Chris unwraps a fortune cookie near his plate and reads the tiny slip of paper aloud. "Ethan will be in the top five for sure."

"Very funny." I smile. "Let me see that."

He moves it out of my reach. "What does yours say?"

"Doesn't matter." The truth is, I don't want to know. What if it says, "Better luck next time," or "Win some, lose some"? I break open my cookie and put the fortune in my pocket without looking at it.

After dinner, there's a one-man show and a lecture on stage presentation, which is way cooler than it sounds. Then Chris and I go back to our room. It's been an incredible day, but it feels good to collapse onto my hotel bed.

While Chris takes a shower, I call home.

"Did the judges like the candy?" Freddy always starts with the most important thing. "Do you have a big TV in your room? Did you get to meet Magnus?"

"Yes, yes, and he's not here."

"Are you in the top five?"

"I won't know 'til tomorrow afternoon."

"Don't worry. I know you will be."

"Thanks, Freddy."

"Daddy wants to say hi."

"Hey there," Dad says. "How is Atlantic City treating you?"

"Great. Really great! How's everything there? How's Jake?"

"So far so good. He's getting stronger every day."

We talk a few more minutes, then he wishes me luck and we hang up. I wonder how much luck has to do with it. What about practicing for hours and hours? What about wanting something so much it's almost all you think about?

Chris's hair is damp from the shower. He yawns and falls onto his bed. "If you want to stay up and read or watch TV, it won't bother me. I slept through three fire drills last semester."

"Thanks. I think I'll just go over my act in my head."

"Sleep well, Ethan. I know you'll be awesome tomorrow."

"Thanks. I'm really glad you're here."

"Me too." He turns out the light and rolls onto his stomach.

I stay on my back and stare at the ceiling. The room is dark, but my head is filled with pictures: Magnus dazzling an audience; colorful magicians in the lobby; Amazing Amelia performing her close-up act; the judges smiling when Chris calls out the right card from his seat.

Then I close my eyes and picture something that hasn't happened—at least, not yet: the huge theater is full, the audience hushed with anticipation and excitement. The judge leans into the microphone and says, "The winner of this year's Junior Competition is . . ." He pauses and the entire audience holds its breath. Then he smiles, opens the envelope, and reads the name on the card: "Ethan Miller!"

I jump out of my seat, give Chris a high five, and race up to the stage.

I play the whole thing over in my mind, again and again. And again. Maybe, if I play it over enough times, it really will come true.

CHAPTER TWENTY-FIVE

I'm already awake as the alarm sounds. I take the world's fastest shower, throw on jeans and the silver-and-black Magic Fest T-shirt all the junior magicians got, and head downstairs with Chris for the breakfast buffet.

"Mind if we join you?"

I look up to see Amazing Amelia and her mom. "Not at all."

"You were great yesterday." Amelia puts down a tray loaded with food.

"Thanks. You too." I stare at the omelet, waffles, fruit, and bacon on her plate.

She smiles. "What can I say? Competing makes me hungry."

"Not me. I've barely eaten since I left Maryland."

"You two had yourselves a road trip, then," her mom says. "We're lucky. We live twenty minutes from here, so our whole family can see the show."

"Yeah, so lucky." Amelia smiles. "Everyone can come and embarrass me."

"Well, it's only fifteen dollars a seat for the big show," her mom explains. "And your dad really wants to see you up on that stage."

"Assuming I make the top five," Amelia reminds her.

"Oh, you will." Amelia's mom tousles her hair. "I believe in you."

I feel a stab of homesickness and wish *my* mom were here with me. And Dad. And Jake. Even Freddy (though I'd never tell him that).

Amelia and I spend the rest of breakfast comparing notes on our fellow magicians. We jump when a voice booms over an intercom: "Attention all junior magicians. The close-up results have been posted outside the Dealer's Room."

Forty-three junior magicians, including Amelia and me, race down the hall and around the corner. It takes forever for the people in front of us to check out the list. Most of them walk away with frowns and slumped shoulders, but a couple grin and high-five each other. Amelia looks at me and crosses her fingers. "Good luck."

"You too."

The line finally clears and we get to the list.

"I can't believe it!" she cries. "We're tied for first place!"

I stare at the list. At the thirty-seven out of forty points we both earned. The second-highest scorer is thirty-five.

Before I can yell or cheer or anything, Amelia looks me in the eye with a mischievous grin. "Don't think I'm gonna go easy on you, King of Chaos."

"Bring it, Amazing Amelia." I smile back.

There's just enough time before the stage acts start for me to make a phone call home.

"Did you win?" Freddy asks.

"Not yet. But it's going pretty well so far. Is Mom or Dad around?"

"Uh-huh."

"Ethan? Is everything all right?" Mom asks.

"Everything's great. I'm tied for first place after the close-up competition."

"That's wonderful!" I can hear a huge smile in her voice.

"Thanks. How's Jake doing?"

"Much better. He should be home by the time you're back tomorrow. Daddy and I are going to see him as soon as Emma and Bubba show up to watch Freddy."

"Give him a hug for me."

"Will do. Call us after the stage act, okay?"

"I will. And Mom? Thanks for letting me come."

"I'm glad it all worked out."

"Me too. I just . . . I wish you all were here with me."

"We are," she says.

And I realize that she's right.

I think about Bubba giving me my first magic kit; Ms. Carlin's hands flying around as we come up with the name for my act; Freddy grinning after I teach him the crayon trick; my parents applauding after my practice rehearsal; and Jake watching my one-handed shuffle.

I want to win so badly . . . for them, and for me.

———————

Everything I've been working at and practicing over the past months has led to this moment.

I adjust my cape for the zillionth time. My props wait on the table at center stage. Every inch of me trembles. My throat is dry again. My brain is going crazy. My heart beats way too fast.

"Let's give a warm welcome to our next contestant, eleven-year-old Ethan Miller, The King of Chaos!"

I touch the red crinkly paper in my pocket and take a deep breath. This is it.

The spotlight wraps me in a surreal glow. I nod to the guy backstage, and the familiar music of Scott Joplin's "The Entertainer" fills the room and helps put me in the magic zone. I make a dignified bow and my top hat falls off, revealing a gold crown underneath. I hold up a huge, glittery sign with letters all jumbled up, then turn it around to the unscrambled side: THE KING OF CHAOS.

I start off my act with one mini marshmallow and three silver cups on a small table. As I shuffle them around, one marshmallow becomes two, two turn into three, and three become four. The music speeds up, and I begin to juggle them. Then I pop the marshmallows into my mouth, rub my stomach, and four more appear in my hand out of nowhere. With a wave of my wand, they turn into one large pink marshmallow.

I make a face, like "Huh?" Then shrug and pop it into my mouth. I start to move the cups out of the way, when another little marshmallow appears, and another . . . I pop them into my mouth—except I miss one! It dive-bombs straight onto the stage floor.

I can't believe it. This never happened at home. I practiced a trillion times, and it always worked. The lively, happy music keeps going, but I don't. My body freezes while my mind races like crazy, trying to figure out what to do. Keep going? Run offstage and hide somewhere? Pretend nothing went wrong?

Pretend, like Freddy does . . .

"Oops?" I say.

To my surprise, the audience laughs!

I pick the fallen marshmallow off the floor and look at it,

like I'm debating whether to eat it or not. I shrug and put it in my left pocket. Then I take another marshmallow from my right pocket and eat that instead, then continue where I left off. I decide to drop another one on purpose, and say "Oops" again, hoping the audience will think it's all part of my act—and they laugh again!

I pop the last one into my mouth, but something is wrong. I make a face and pull a brown egg (hard-boiled this time) out of my mouth. With a shrug, I start to juggle it, along with two of the silver cups. The music gets faster again, and so does my juggling. The second the last note sounds, I "drop" the egg into my top hat. I look inside, make a disgusted face like it's cracked open, and pull out a rubber chicken.

Everything else goes smoothly and I get a lot of applause at the end, so I guess it worked.

I just don't know if it worked enough to make the top five.

CHAPTER TWENTY-SIX

"I can't believe it!" Amelia and I shout in unison.

Thirty-eight magicians are going home disappointed, not getting the chance to perform again tonight . . . but not Amelia. And not me. We both made the top five!

She steps toward me and for a second I'm afraid she's going to hug me or something. Luckily, at the last second, she reaches out and we do a high five.

There's just enough time for Chris and me to celebrate with a quick pizza (one slice is all I can manage) before I need to get ready for the main event. I wonder if Amelia is as excited—and terrified—as I am. Somehow I doubt it. She seems so cool and collected all the time. It probably helps that she's got her family here for support.

I've been trying to call *my* family since I found out about making the top five, but no one answers. Not even their cell phones. I'm starting to get a bad feeling. . . .

It's almost time to go. I'm supposed to be backstage forty-five minutes before the show. But I really need to talk to Mom or Dad. Even Freddy would make me feel better at this point.

I try one last time, but Mom's phone just rings and rings. I can't even leave a voice message because the box is full.

"I don't know why no one's answering," I say.

"Why don't you try your grandparents?" Chris asks.

"Good idea." I dial the number and wait. One ring, two rings, three . . . I'm about to give up when I hear Freddy's voice on the other end.

"Freddy? Guess what? I'm in the top five! And my friend, Amazing Amelia, is, too!" I pause to take a breath and wait to hear him let out a shout of congratulations.

But it's quiet on the other end. Too quiet.

"Freddy? Where is everybody? I tried calling all afternoon, but—"

"I'm not supposed to tell you," he says.

"Tell me what?"

"About Jake . . ."

My stomach twists itself into a knot and my throat goes dry. "What about him?"

"Freddy?" I hear Emma's voice. "Who is it?"

"Ethan."

"Give me the phone," I hear her say. "Hello, Ethan?"

"What's going on with Jake?"

"How's Magic Fest?" she asks, dodging my question.

"How's Jake?"

There's a long pause. "He . . . had a setback. He's back in Intensive Care."

"What? Why didn't anyone call me?"

"You worked so hard to be in the competition. Your mom didn't want to ruin it for you."

I can't believe this is happening. "I need to talk to her, now!"

Emma starts to argue, then gives in and tells me the number for the hospital.

My hands are shaking. The numbers are blurry. It takes me three tries to dial it correctly.

"Hello?" It's Mom. She sounds really tired.

"Mom! What's going on? Is Jake all right?"

"He's hanging on . . ."

"What does that mean?"

"I'll try to call you later, all right?"

"No! I want to know what's happening!"

"Ethan, this isn't a good time. I have to—"

"Wait!"

"Jake loves you. . . ." Her voice cracks.

I wait for more, but her end of the phone has gone quiet. "Mom? Are you there?"

A few seconds pass, then a different voice comes on the phone. "E?"

"Dad? How's Jake?" I wait again, but he doesn't say anything. "Dad. How is—"

"Not good."

"But . . . he's gonna get better, right?" The other end of the line is silent. "I mean, I know he had a setback, but . . . he's gonna be okay. Right? He's Super Jake. . . ."

"I don't know."

"What do you mean you don't know?" I can barely get the words out. Every inch of me feels sick.

"I'm sorry. . . ."

"There must be something I can do to help!"

"I wish there were, but all any of us can do is wait and see. . . ."

But I don't want to wait.

I can't.

Dad tells me he loves me and hangs up and my throat hurts and my cheeks are wet and—

"Hey." Chris has my gold crown in his hand. "We have to go," he says softly.

My eyes are on the crown . . . but my fingers are wrapped around Jake's crinkly paper. "Yeah," I tell him. "We do."

I grab my suitcase.

"What are you doing?" Chris asks.

"Jake needs me."

"We can leave the minute this is over," Chris says, still holding my crown.

He's right. We could. After all this work and all this time, I'm so close. I actually have a chance to win this whole thing.

But what about Jake? What are his chances?

If I wait, like Dad said—it could be too late.

"No," I tell Chris. "We have to go now."

It's hard to believe four hours ago I was in Atlantic City, and now I'm about to walk into a hospital, not knowing what I'll find or how Jake will be.

Before Chris and I left the competition, I went backstage and told the first judge I saw that I was leaving because of a family emergency. She was really nice about it, and I was doing okay . . . until I saw Amazing Amelia.

"Why aren't you in costume?" she asked.

I looked at her, all dressed up in a tuxedo and top hat. "My little brother is really sick and I need to be with him."

She took a step toward me and, instead of a high five, this time she hugged me. And I hugged her back.

Hospitals are usually depressing, but this one is different. Like Chris explained, it's for children only. Everywhere I look, I see cheerful drawings on the walls, bears on the ceilings, and happy colors everywhere. There's even a high school band performing in the lobby. I hope Jake hears the music; the trumpets might make him feel more at home.

Wherever I look there are kids: in baby carriers and strollers, on crutches, in wheelchairs. . . .

"Are they all sick like Jake?" I whisper.

"I dunno," Chris says. "I hope not."

We follow the signs down one corridor and up another, then around a corner to a bank of elevators. Chris pushes the up button. When the doors open, there's already a family inside: a mom, a dad, and a skinny little kid around Freddy's age, with big brown eyes, a friendly smile, and a pole with an IV. I try not to stare at him, but I can't help it. He stares at me, too, then waves and gives a shy smile. I smile back.

The doors open again, and Chris and I head down a long hallway with rainbows and teddy bears and big red hearts. I feel my own heart beating extra hard and fast, and think how scared Jake must've been all this time. I mean, it seems like a nice place and all; it's just that home is so much nicer.

We stop at a set of double doors and Chris presses a buzzer. After a minute or two, Mom and Dad come through the doors. Mom gives us each a hug. Her lips are smiling but her eyes are sad, and her clothes are all wrinkled, like she slept in them.

"Where's Jake?" I ask.

"He's with Freddy and your grandparents," Dad says.

"You'll see him soon," Mom says. She bites her lip and looks at Dad.

"We want to talk to you first." Dad looks at Chris.

"How about I go visit with Jake?" Chris says.

Mom asks one of the nurses to show him the way, then she and Dad take me to a little room barely big enough for the three of us, with just a table and some chairs.

"We know how badly you want to see Jake. He wants to see you, too. . . ." Mom breaks off and looks at Dad again.

"The thing is," Dad says, "he might not look the way you expect. He's hooked up to machines, and his eyes are shut, and . . ." His voice cracks and his eyes get watery.

My stomach muscles tighten and my throat feels like it's closing up.

We sit in silence for a while. Finally, Dad gets up and leads us back to the double doors. He presses the buzzer and the big doors swing open. I follow them through a maze of beds separated by nothing but thin curtains. There are doctors wearing serious expressions and nurses who smile at us. We come to a stop at one curtain, and Mom says, "Jake, guess who's here?"

One look is enough to explain everything Mom and Dad couldn't.

Jake's under a fuzzy green blanket I don't recognize, and all I can see are his face and feet. His socks are off, and a thing with a little red light is attached to one of his toes. His eyes are closed and he's really pale. There's a big piece of tape across his face. And a tube in his mouth.

Freddy runs over to me. "You came!" He puts his scrawny arms around me and I hug him back.

I hear Mom crying and feel my own tears, hot and wet, streaming down my cheeks. I let go of Freddy. "Jake's gonna get better, right?"

"The doctors and nurses are doing all they can," Dad says.

"Look, Ethan!" Freddy runs back to Jake. "I think he's smiling!"

My legs feel wobbly, and my stomach is killing me, but I walk over to the side of Jake's bed.

"See? See him smiling?" Freddy says.

I take Jake's pudgy hand and squeeze it the way he likes. "Hey, Super Jake," I whisper. I bend over and hug him as close as I can with all the wires and stuff. He feels warm and soft and cuddly like always.

I want to lie down next to him.

I want to leave this horrible place and never come back.

But not without Jake.

CHAPTER TWENTY-SEVEN

The absolute last place I want to be is at school.

First period, in band, I play more wrong notes than right ones. By the time the bell rings, I drag myself to my locker and get the combination wrong more times than I can count.

Daniel's at my side, eyeing me like I just got back from Mars. "You okay, dude?"

Brian shows up on my other side, smiling. "What music were you playing in class today?"

I want to tell them what happened, only it's hard to know where to start. My brain is tired and the hallway is noisy and if I start talking I might never stop. So I mumble something about having to get to science class and leave before they can ask anything else.

——————

I don't even know what happens in the next two classes—

hopefully nothing important because I completely zone out in each. When I get to lunch, the last thing I want to do is eat. Or talk.

"So, how was Magic Fest?" Daniel asks.

"Yeah, what happened? Did you get to meet Magnus?" Brian asks.

Should I say how incredible it was? How great it was hanging out with Chris? How much fun I had with Amelia? Should I talk about how the judges applauded my close-up act? How exciting it was to see my name at the top of the list? How surreal it felt to be one of the top five magicians?

I want to, but then I'd have to explain why I left early and tell them about the hospital and Jake, and I *don't* want to talk about that.

"It was okay." I force myself to take a bite of my sandwich and chew a really long time so I don't have to talk.

But that's not enough for Daniel. "'It was *okay*'? Are you kidding me? Dude! This is all you've been talking about for, like, the past four months. And all you say is—"

"I feel sick," I blurt out. And that, at least, is the truth.

I run out to the hall and throw up in the closest trash can.

By the time I get to math class, the only numbers I care about are how many hours it's been since I've seen Jake, and how many more 'til I see him again.

"Ethan!" The way Miss Wright glares at me, I can tell she's called my name more than once. "What is the value of x?" She points at the whiteboard.

I shrug and keep doodling in my binder. All I want is to go home and find out if Jake is okay. Maybe Ms. Carlin will let me leave seventh period a little early. . . .

"It might help if you look at the problem on the board," she says.

I look, then shrug again.

"Ethan, at least make an effort. Try and figure out—"

"I don't care!"

Miss Wright's eyes get huge. "Excuse me?"

"I don't care. It doesn't mean anything. You wanna know the value of x so badly? You figure it out!"

Miss Wright ushers me out of the classroom while the assistant teacher tries to settle the rest of the class, but it's pretty out of control thanks to my outburst. Classmates are talking and laughing and shaking their heads. . . . I don't know how she's going to calm them down.

You'd think Miss Wright would be mad, but once we are in the hallway, she just looks at me with The Face—and I real- ize she knows about Jake. Of course she does. My father is the assistant principal after all.

"Ethan," she says, "I know this is a difficult time, so I'm

willing to overlook what just happened. But next time, I'll have to hold you accountable, understood? Otherwise, your peers will start misbehaving."

I just look at her. I have nothing to say.

She sighs. "Look, I'm not going to call your parents at a time like—"

"That's a great idea!" I smile for the first time all day.

Her eyes open even wider. "What is?"

"Calling my parents." I turn around and head toward the office without another word.

———————————

"Where are you?" Mom asks when she hears my voice on the phone.

"I'm at school. How's Jake?"

"A little better, but still pretty sick. You know Jake, though. He's . . ."

". . . a fighter," we say together. Then, for a few seconds, neither of us says anything at all.

"Mom? Will you give him a hug for me?"

The other end of the line is silent.

". . . Mom?"

"Of course I will." I hear her sniffle. "I'm sorry, sweetie, the nurse is calling me. I need to—"

"Go," we say at the same time.

I'm late to English class but I have a pass from Miss Wright, who was nicer to me than I expected. Usually, no matter how bad the rest of the day might be, I feel better once I'm in English class. But not today.

Normally, I raise my hand so much that Ms. Carlin laughs and asks me to let someone else talk; today, I don't raise my hand or open my mouth once. Even Ned notices something's off. He scribbles a note and passes it to me, asking if I'm okay. All I can do is shrug.

Finally, the last bell rings. I grab my stuff and head for the door.

"Ethan?" It's Ms. Carlin. She looks really worried about something; turns out it's me. "I heard about Jake. Do you want to stay and talk?"

"No, I need to go home and find out what's going on."

She nods, then steps toward me and puts her hand on my shoulder. "If there's anything I can do . . ."

I have to get out now, before I lose it.

After I get home, there's another disaster.

Chris and his mom had to go somewhere, so Tina and I met Freddy at his bus stop then we all walked back to our house. Only it doesn't feel like home right now.

I grab three apples and start juggling, just to be doing

something.

"You've gotten a lot better." Tina smiles at me.

"Thanks."

"Ugh! I wish it would come out already!" Freddy yanks at the loose tooth he's been complaining about all week.

"Here, maybe this'll help." I toss an apple his way.

"I bet taffy would work better! Or bubble gum!" Since no one takes him up on this, he keeps going. "When Jake has his first loose tooth, will we give him an apple?"

Tina and I look at each other, pretty sure the answer is no.

"Try brushing your teeth and see if that helps it fall out," I tell him.

He drags himself down the hall.

"So, guess what?" Tina asks as I take a bite out of one of the apples. "Remember at Jake's party, when we started talking about the fund-raiser?"

I nod and take another bite.

"And remember how I thought maybe my school's jazz band would play? I spoke with the band teacher today, and he was totally down for it. Then, while I was standing there, the chorus teacher came in and said the show choir would be happy to help out, too."

"Wow. That's pretty awesome."

She smiles. "I know, right?"

"Look!" Freddy races in, a small, bloody tooth in his hand. You'd think he won an Olympic gold medal or something.

"Congratulations!" Tina cries. "How'd it come out?"

"I sneezed." He plops down onto the sofa.

Tina laughs, then says, "Remember when Jake got his first tooth?"

I nod. "I was the one who discovered it."

"You were! We all knew something was going on 'cause Jake was being fussy during his feedings."

"And Jake is *never* fussy during his feedings," Freddy says.

I smile at him. "I remember I put my finger in his mouth, and all of a sudden I felt this little bump."

"And you called to tell me." Tina smiles like it's the best memory ever.

Freddy jumps up. "I've got to put my tooth under my pillow for the tooth fairy!" He races down the hall to his room.

Uh-oh. I look at Tina, panicking. "What'll we do? Mom always does the tooth fairy stuff."

"We'll figure something out. It can't be that hard. Just stick a dollar under his pillow when he's not looking."

"No, that's not enough! Mom always leaves a note. Y'know, a letter? From the tooth fairy. And Freddy keeps them. Every one. He'll see the writing doesn't match! I've gotta call Mom!"

I jump up and dial the hospital number while Tina distracts Freddy. It takes forever for her to pick up.

"Yes?" Mom answers.

"Freddy sneezed and his tooth came out."

"I can't talk right now—"

"But this is an emergency."

"That is *not* an emergency!" she yells into the phone. "Ethan, do you have any idea what's going on here?"

I can't believe she's yelling at me, and I don't mean to yell back, but the words just fly out: "How could I? No one tells me anything!"

"I don't have time for this. One of the doctors is here." Then she hangs up on me.

She's never done that. Ever. Not even that time in third grade when I threw wood chips during recess and got a citation and the secretary called Mom and I got in big trouble.

I storm off to my room and slam the door.

I need to think about something else. I go to my bookcase and look for a book I haven't read. The top shelf is fantasy; the second is science fiction and books with magic tricks; the third is mysteries; the fourth is stuff Mom read to me when I was little. Sometimes, I pick one out and read it to Freddy: *Peter Pan*; *The Wizard of Oz*; *Winnie-the-Pooh*....

All of a sudden, there's a different Pooh book I want to see:

one I've never read. I go to Jake's room and flip on his Snoopy light switch. Everything looks the same: light-up toys scattered on the floor, picture books on the shelf, Looney Tunes stickers on the wall, stuffed animals all over the bed. Everything just waiting for him.

I take the book off the shelf, sit down on his little bed, and look through the autographs:

It's wonderful to be at your birthday party!! You look very handsome.

—Emma

Hi, buddy! You are my "bestest" little eating guy—you make me look good! I love your smile that we worked so hard to get. Saying "Mama" is our next big job! I love you very much, my cuddly boy.

—Mandy

Jake, you are lucky to have two brothers who enjoy discovering how your toys work as much as you do!

—Suzette

Jake, you have taught many of us how to cel-
ebrate the seemingly little things in life, that
have become so significant. I thank you and
celebrate the sweet boy you are.

—Mrs. Todd

My eyes are watering. Maybe this isn't a good idea. I look around Jake's bed and see Ninja Bear half-hidden under the blanket. I pick him up and throw him across the room the way Jake and I do.

That makes me feel better. I pick up the Pooh book again.

Happy birthday, Jake. Lots of people love
you. Especially me. :)

—Tina

And, my favorite:

Jake—you bring out the best in people.

—Mr. Todd

I close the book, then shut my eyes and imagine Jake here, next to me. . . .

"Hey! What are you doing in here?"

I open my eyes and see Freddy staring at me. My legs ache from being squished in Jake's little bed. The rest of me doesn't feel so great, either.

"Guess what? Daddy called and he's coming home!"

I want to get up, but it's nice and peaceful here (except for Freddy). He puts his hand on my arm, leans over so I feel his little kid breath on my face, and says, "It's okay. Sometimes I fall asleep in here, too."

"Oh yeah? I wonder what Jake would say if he knew we were sleeping in his bed?" Before Freddy can answer, I pull him on top of me and tickle him. It feels good to hear him laugh.

Soon, we hear Tina saying hi to Dad, so we head down the hall to see him waving two boxes in the air. "Did somebody order pizza?"

Tina takes the boxes and Dad pulls Freddy and me in for a hug.

"I have missed you guys." His voice sounds funny and he's holding onto us longer and harder than usual.

Freddy pulls out of the hug first. "Look! I lost my tooth!"

While Dad fusses over him, Tina sets the table and asks me to grab a few things for a salad. I search the fridge and discover that the milk is sour; we're out of orange juice; the carrots are slimy; the cucumbers are mushy; and the bag of lettuce is brown and all-around gross.

I grab a pen to write on Mom's grocery list. To save time, she has a bunch of ready-made lists for stuff we get every week, like milk, bread, and baby food. Then Freddy and I add the important things, like chips and cookies. I scribble *food* on the paper.

"Who's hungry?" Dad serves up the top box.

Freddy attacks his slice like he hasn't eaten in weeks.

"How's Jake?" I ask as Dad hands me a glass of iced tea.

He looks over at Freddy, then raises his eyebrows at Tina.

"Freddy," Tina says, "how about we make this extra fun and eat in front of the TV?"

He doesn't have to be asked twice. Freddy races to the TV room and Tina follows.

It's just the two of us now. I look at Dad's unshaven face and bloodshot eyes, and my stomach starts to hurt again.

I take a deep breath. Then, for the second time, ask "How's Jake?"

———————————

"Whaddaya mean, he's not gagging? Isn't that good?" I ask. We've been sitting in the kitchen so long, the pizza's cold and the iced tea is warm, but I still don't understand what's going on.

"It's complicated," Dad explains. "Right now, he's being fed intravenously."

"Through that needle in his arm?"

"Right. Which is okay, for a while. For Jake to take a bottle again, though, he needs to get his gag reflex back, so he can cough without choking."

"Well, he had one before, right? It's not like it just ran off and disappeared."

Dad takes a deep breath, then slowly lets it out. "Ethan, Jake's temperature got up to one hundred and seven."

"What? How could that happen?"

He doesn't answer right away; when he does, his voice is soft and gentle. "Did you know that when Jake was born, a nurse told me babies like him don't last a year? He's already lasted twice that. You know why?"

"He's a fighter."

"That, and because we've taken such good care of him. All of us. But sometimes. . . ."

We sit there a minute, saying nothing. "He could still get his gag reflex back, though, right?" I ask.

"Technically."

"What's that supposed to mean?"

Dad studies his plate like it holds the secret to the universe. "The doctors say it's very unlikely after this long."

"But not impossible, right?"

"No, Ethan. Nothing's impossible. Jake has taught us that."

Before I go to sleep that night, I pray for the first time in a long time. I know God's busy and everything, so I get right to the point: "Please, God, let Jake cough."

CHAPTER TWENTY-EIGHT

"Ethan, look! Look at me!"

I glance up from the humongous sandcastle I'm building, prepared to protect it from Freddy-the-Destroyer, and can't believe what I see. Jake is dancing in and out of the waves, jumping and giggling and calling my name.

I race toward him, water splashing me in the face. I throw my arms around him and we hold on to each other.

"Look at you!" I swing him around, spinning and laughing.

"What's so funny?" Someone is tapping on my shoulder.

"Huh?" I mumble, still staring at Jake as he fades away. "Wait! Come back! Don't go!"

"What are you talking about? I'm right here!"

I open my eyes to see Freddy in my room, instead of Jake in the ocean.

"Ethan, someone's at the door."

"What time is it?"

"The big hand is on the . . ."

"Never mind." I lean over and squint at my clock. It's almost 1:00 a.m. There's a storm outside, so loud I don't know how I slept through it. The doorbell rings. "Where's Dad?"

"I dunno!" Freddy cries. "I looked everywhere!"

"All right, take it easy." I flick on the hall light and make my way to the door, Freddy so close behind he's practically in front of me. I hit the porch light and stand on my tiptoes.

"It's Mrs. Todd." I open the door, wondering what's going on.

She comes in, her raincoat and umbrella dripping water onto the floor. "Is your dad around?" she asks. No trace of a smile or a "Sorry I woke you."

"I think so."

"Could you get him for me?"

I nod and leave her in the hall with Freddy. "Dad?" I check all the bedrooms and bathrooms. Where can he be? Would he leave without telling us? Maybe he went to the hospital to see Mom and Jake . . . in the middle of the night? I run down to the basement, still trying to make sense of things.

Then I see him—sound asleep on the sofa, book open across his chest, glasses still on his face.

"Dad?"

He opens his eyes and looks around, like he doesn't know where he is. "Ethan? What's wrong?"

"I dunno. Mrs. Todd is upstairs and—"

He jumps off the sofa and takes the stairs two at a time. I race after him.

"Rebecca called from the hospital," Mrs. Todd says before Dad can even ask. "The phones are down because of the storm, and she couldn't reach you on your cell."

"I must've forgotten to charge it," Dad says. "Thank you for coming over."

"No problem."

Without another word, he goes down the hall. I hear a door close.

"Who wants cocoa?" Mrs. Todd offers with a weird smile. Like maybe if she smiles wide enough, it will seem perfectly normal for her to be in our house in the middle of the night. Like that's gonna fool anyone.

"I do!" Freddy grins like an idiot.

"What's going on?" I ask.

"I really don't know." Mrs. Todd fills the kettle with water and places it on the stovetop.

"Is Jake okay?" I clench my fingers into fists.

She gently puts her hands on my shoulders. "Let's wait and hear what your dad says, all right?" Before I can answer, she says, "Freddy, why don't you grab some spoons and napkins? And Ethan, could you get the mugs?"

Dad comes back just as the kettle gives off a really shrill whistle that makes my skin crawl. He looks terrible.

He and Mrs. Todd walk to the door together. They speak so quietly I can only make out the last two words Dad says: ". . . tomorrow morning?"

"Of course," Mrs. Todd replies. Dad thanks her and helps her with her coat and umbrella, then watches as she heads back out into the storm. When she gets across the street, he shuts the door. I follow him into the kitchen and watch him pour hot water into our mugs.

"Is Jake dead?" Freddy blurts out.

"Geez, Freddy! Shut up!" I yell, my heart pounding. "Of course he's not dead, you stupid jerk!"

"Daddy! He called me a—"

"Jake is not dead. But he did have another setback."

Freddy slurps his cocoa. He's acting all happy, like he's settling in for a bedtime story.

"How can you drink at a time like this?" I shout.

"I'm thirsty," he says in a very quiet voice.

I push my mug as far away as I can. The lump in my throat makes it impossible for liquid to go down. I feel my eyes tear up, but I'm too mad to cry. "No one ever tells me anything!"

"Me neither," Freddy says.

I'm about to yell at him some more, then I notice tears streaking down his cheeks, and I feel even worse.

Dad sighs. "I'm sorry, guys. I know things are tough right now. And I don't have a lot of answers. All I can tell you is the doctors are working very hard to help Jake."

"Can we see him?" I ask.

"Not right now," Dad says. "I'm going there in a few hours, and—"

I already know the rest of his sentence. "We're going to the Todds', right?"

He reaches out and puts Freddy's hand in one of his and mine in the other. "Do you remember the very first time Jake came home? He had a monitor that would beep if he stopped breathing, a gigantic oxygen tank, and an NG tube that went up his nose and down to his stomach."

"The Energy tube?" Freddy asks.

"Exactly." Dad gives him a small smile. "Your mom and I asked you to be gentle because he was very fragile."

"Then you told us he was a fighter," I say, remembering. "And he might get rid of all that stuff later on."

Dad nods. "And he did, too. Every single thing."

I think about how far Jake has come since then, and how hard he tries. If anyone can beat the odds, it's Super Jake.

CHAPTER TWENTY-NINE

A few hours later, we're back at the Todds' house.

"I'm ready for another pancake!" Freddy tells Mrs. Todd.

"Here." I dump mine onto his plate as the doorbell rings. Chris answers the door, then calls my name.

I head down the hall, wondering if it's Daniel or Brian. Turns out it's neither.

"Hey," Ned says. "I heard Jake's in the hospital. . . ." He looks at his feet. "Is he . . . will he be okay?"

I don't know what to say, so I shrug.

"I got something for him." Ned reaches into his backpack. "I thought maybe he'd like it." He hands me a plastic Daffy Duck. "It squeaks. See?" He squeezes it.

"Thanks." I want to say more. I want to tell him Jake would really like it and that I'm glad *he* likes Jake—that now he sees him for who he is. But the words don't come.

"Oh. I almost forgot." He pulls out a wrinkled paper filled with colorful squiggles and princess stickers. "It's from Wendy. For Jake."

There's so much I want to say, only my throat's too tight, so I just nod.

"Well. I better get to school."

I nod again.

He turns to go but looks back over his shoulder at me. "Tell Jake to feel better soon."

I'm super late to band, but the teacher just smiles at me. I make it to the rest of my classes on time. Except it's like I'm not really there. Sometimes I'm seeing Jake hooked up to tubes and covered with that green blanket. Sometimes we're wrestling on the living room couch or hurling Ninja Bear across the room together. I even come up with a new Food Island story during math class. Jake would really like it because he rescues Wendy and they have a tea party at the end.

When I get home, the blue minivan is in our driveway. I sprint to the door and Dad wraps me in a bear hug.

"You're here! Is Jake doing better?"

Dad shakes his head. "He's still in Intensive Care, E. Mom and I came home to spend a little time with you and Freddy."

"Where is she?"

"In bed, resting for a bit."

"Oh."

I follow him into the kitchen and watch him fix a mug of coffee. "Can I make you a snack?" he asks.

"No, thanks." I haven't had much of an appetite lately. I want to talk more about Jake, but before I figure out what to ask, Dad puts his hand on my shoulder.

"I need to make some phone calls, E. But later on, maybe you can show me some card tricks or we could watch something on TV?"

"Sure, sounds good."

He squeezes my shoulder, grabs his mug of coffee, and goes downstairs. I stand there a second then head to my room. On the way, I stop by Jake's room. It feels so empty without him. I sit on his little bed and I miss him and I wish he was here. I wish I'd spent more time playing with him and stretching him and telling him Food Island stories.

Most of all, I wish wishes really came true.

———————

Dad makes dinner but Mom doesn't eat.

I don't eat much, either.

When Freddy asks her to play a game, she says not right now.

I don't feel like playing, either, but when Dad asks me to

join Freddy and him for some board games, I do anyway. After, I finish my homework and take a shower.

When I come out of the bathroom, the house is spooky quiet. I start to wonder if everyone left and forgot to tell me. But when I peek in Freddy's room he's on the floor, hard at work with crayons and magic markers.

"What are you making?"

"A picture for Mommy to take to Jakey tomorrow," he answers without looking up.

I see my parents' bedroom light on. I'm about to knock when I hear her say something about Jake coming home.

Maybe he's doing better! I press my ear against the door to eavesdrop.

"I don't think it's a good idea," Dad says. "It's not fair to the boys. . . ."

"Fair?" Mom whisper-yells. "What does fair have to do with any of this?"

For a minute it's quiet, then Dad says, "Maybe we should get some sleep. It's hard to think straight when you're exhausted."

"It's hard to think straight when your son is dying," Mom says.

I feel like someone kicked me in the stomach.

I can't breathe.

Can't think.

I take one step, then another, a zombie retreating down the hallway.

I go to my room and close the door behind me. It's a big mess, except for my magic trick props. Every container is carefully organized and color-coded: the blue has my oldest tricks; the yellow's got all the cards; the orange has coins. Looking through them always makes me feel better.

I pull out a few tricks, only they're too easy; I need something challenging. I look through the sets of cards and find my favorite deck. It's got gold edges and a picture of a real Swiss castle.

I shuffle the cards with my left hand, then take a deep breath and try with my right. They fly all over my bed and onto the floor. I sweep them up and try again. And again. I can't do it.

I can't do it without Super Jake.

I look at the cards on my bed, the boxes of other props splayed out on the floor—they're all worthless. Who cares about this junk? Trick decks and fake thumbs and plastic wands. Tooth fairies and Ninja Bear and Food Island. Pixie dust and make-believe.

Like making believe Jake's gonna be okay.

I gather the cards to put them back in the box. I've got about half the deck in my hands then look at the other half, scattered all over the floor. Then I make a decision.

I dump the half deck into my trash can, then pick up the rest from the floor and throw them in after.

I'm just getting started.

And it feels good.

My eyes search the room for my next trash can victim. My hands reach out and grab the yellow box. I turn it upside down and all my other card decks tumble into the trash.

Good riddance.

I stare at the empty container for a few seconds, trying to decide if it's worth keeping.

I toss it in after the cards.

My trash can's getting pretty full. I go to my closet and yank out a huge plastic bag I use for overnights and empty the can's contents into it.

I grab the blue box next and it all spills out: sponge animals and metal rings and green plastic balls and a red scarf that changes colors and I throw every single thing into the bag.

I'm sick of them all.

I'm glad they're gone.

I'm about to grab my orange box when I see a "Miller's Magic" flyer on the floor and I grab that instead, ripping it in half again and again 'til the pieces are too small to rip anymore. Then I throw them into the bag. I'm breathing hard and sweating and my stomach is cramping, but I don't stop.

It doesn't matter. Nothing matters.

I turn back to grab the orange box when, out of the corner of my eye, I see my wand and top hat sitting on the shelf. They fooled so many people for so long . . . me most of all.

I throw the top hat to the floor and kick it. "I hate you!" I kick it again. "I HATE YOU!" I stomp on it again and again until, finally, it collapses like a dead dream.

"What're you doing?"

I look up and see Freddy, but he's kind of blurry. "What's it look like?" I rub my watery eyes with the back of my hand.

He's staring at me like I've gone nuts. "Your top hat. All your magic tricks!"

"It's over." I wipe my face and grab the smashed top hat and shove it into the bag, along with the rest.

"What's over?"

I tie the bag and lug it toward the door. "Everything. Dumb tricks, stupid shows . . ."

He blocks my way. "What if you change your mind?"

"I won't."

"But what about all the magic—"

"Don't you get it, Freddy? There's no such thing as magic!"

I turn away from his shocked expression, squeeze past him into the hall, and dump the bag into the garbage can.

CHAPTER THIRTY

It's morning. We're sitting around the breakfast table like everything's fine. Like *Jake's* gonna be fine.

Like I still believe in magic.

"Dad and I are going to spend the night with Jake." Mom adds a second waffle to my plate before I even touch the first. "So, after school go to—"

"The Todds'," I interrupt.

The phone rings. Mom and Dad stare at it, neither moving.

"I'll get it!" Freddy jumps up, but Dad intercepts him and Mom grabs the phone, holding it like a snake about to bite.

"Hello?" she holds her breath, then her shoulders relax. "Oh, hi, Rox. I'm sure Jake misses Wendy, too." Mom steps into the other room so we don't have to watch her cry.

The last bell rings and the school day is finally over. I'm gathering my stuff when Ms. Carlin sits down next to me.

"Do you have a minute?" she asks.

"Sure." It's not like I'm in a big hurry to go to the Todds' house. Again.

"Things aren't going well with Jake, are they?"

I shake my head.

"Would it help to talk about it?"

I shake my head again. We sit there a minute or two. I'm not sure if she wants to say something else, or if she wants me to.

"There is something I've been thinking about," I hear myself say. "Y'know that report on heroes?"

She nods.

"I was thinking, just cuz someone's famous doesn't mean they're a hero. I mean, some famous people are the opposite of heroes. Like Bonnie and Clyde, or Hitler."

"Very true," Ms. Carlin says.

"And some people, who really are heroes, aren't famous at all. Like my grandfather. He gave up five years of his life to fight overseas in World War II. He doesn't talk about it much, but my grandma says he was responsible for the lives of all the soldiers under him and every single one made it home safely."

"That's wonderful. And you're absolutely right, Ethan. He is a hero. You must be proud of him."

"I am. But I think Jake's a hero, too, even though no one will ever hear about him. He can't walk, and he can't talk. He can't even sit up by himself, but he never stops trying...."

Ms. Carlin hands me a tissue, then puts her face right in front of mine and looks at me. Hard. "Listen to me. Jake's a fighter. He could still pull through."

I've been wanting to hear that for days. Now that I finally do, I don't believe it.

———————

When I get to the Todds', Freddy's showing a card trick to Mrs. Todd. It's one of the first I learned, and I taught it to him one day when he was sick and I felt sorry for him. I watch from beside the doorframe, where they can't see me.

"Now put the card back anywhere you want," Freddy instructs her. Mrs. Todd sticks it somewhere in the middle of the deck. Freddy flips through the cards, then picks out one of them. "Is this it?"

Mrs. Todd smiles. "Sure is! Look at that. One day, you're going to be a great magician like your big brother."

"No," Freddy says. "I'll never be as good as Ethan."

"You never know," I say from the doorway.

Freddy grins at me.

The smile on his face makes me feel like, maybe, I've done something right. Mrs. Todd invites me to join them, so the three of us do a few more card tricks and I forget everything for a while. Well, almost.

Once Freddy sits down to work on his homework with Mrs. Todd, I go to the living room to face my own. I start with math, but the only problems on my mind are five minus one equals no Jake.

When I look at the clock again, it's almost six, and the phone hasn't rung yet.

Mrs. Todd calls us for dinner, which is spaghetti.

It's not as good without Jake there to sample the sauce.

———————————

After dinner, Mr. Todd challenges Freddy to a game of checkers, which means Chris and I can escape to the basement to play Monopoly until his mom says it's time for bed. We're almost done putting the money and properties away when Chris stops and looks at me.

"You know, I'm really proud of you."

"Why? I was down to seventy-three dollars and had to mortgage half my properties."

He laughs. "I mean how well you're handling everything. How you've stepped up to help your parents and take care of Freddy."

"Oh." I move the little green houses around so I don't have to look at him. "I dunno."

"Well, I do. And you have. You and Jake have taught me a lot."

I shrug, not knowing what to say. It feels strange to think *I've* taught *Chris.*

I find Mrs. Todd in the living room, sewing a button onto one of Chris's flannel shirts. There's another colossal storm going on, the rain coming down so hard I can't even make out my house across the street.

I wish I were there instead of here. At home when there's a storm, we all sit on the sofa together, watching the lightning and listening to the thunder.

"Is it okay if I stay up awhile?" I ask Mrs. Todd. "Mom always calls when she spends the night away."

"How about you and I chat for a bit?" She puts down the shirt and pats the spot next to her on the sofa.

"So, how are you holding up?" she asks, her voice soft and serious.

I shrug. "I dunno. I miss Jake."

"I know you do."

"I hate sitting around doing nothing."

"You're doing plenty," she says. "Looking out for Freddy, thinking about Jake, loving him. He knows how much you care about him."

"You think so?"

"No doubt about it."

The lights flicker, go out, and come back on. Maybe it's Jake saying hi. Or goodbye.

"Jake will always be your baby brother. Nothing can ever change that." She hugs me tight, then hands me a flashlight, "In case we lose power in the middle of the night."

When I get to our room Freddy's wide awake, sitting cross-legged on the floor with Pita Rabbit by his side. There's a red magic marker in his hand and the rest are scattered all around. From the rainbow on his cheeks and hands, I'd guess he's been drawing for a while.

"Hey, it's way past your bedtime," I say, sitting next to him.

"The storm's too noisy. Besides, I wanted to finish this."

He holds up a poster as big as he is, with fireworks, hearts, and smiley faces all over the place. In the middle, it reads WELCUM HOME JAKE!

"Whaddaya think?" he says.

When I open my mouth to answer, nothing comes out. I feel sick.

"You don't like it?"

"No, it's great."

Just great. Jake's dying, and Freddy thinks he's coming home.

Chris thinks I've got it all under control, but I don't know what I'm doing.

I wish Mom and Dad were here to explain everything, but they're not. I take a deep breath and do my best to "step up."

"Hey, Freddy? How 'bout you put that down for a second?"

He lays down the poster carefully, grabs his bunny, and joins me on the bottom bunk.

"Jake would definitely like the poster . . . but I'm just not sure he's gonna see it."

"How come?"

"Remember when we saw him in the hospital last?"

Freddy nods.

"Remember the tubes and everything? How he couldn't drink from a bottle or eat any food?"

Another nod.

"Well, you know how much Jake loves to eat. So he's thinking about going to Food Island and getting all the pizza and fries he wants."

"Can we go, too?"

I get up from the bed, walk over to the window, and stare at the storm. As bad as it looks, I'd rather be out there than having this conversation.

I'm still trying to figure out how to answer when Freddy says, "I'm sleepy." He and Pita crawl under the covers while

I put the poster and markers away, turn out the light, and pull myself up to the top bunk. The storm's going crazy outside, and my thoughts are going crazy inside my head.

"Ethan? You awake?"

"Yeah."

"Me too. Ethan?"

"Yeah."

"There isn't really a Food Island, is there?"

"No," I whisper into the darkness.

He's quiet for so long, I figure he's either asleep or too upset to talk. What if I said the wrong thing and made everything worse? Maybe I shouldn't have said anything.

"Ethan?"

"Yeah."

"If God is outside, can He hear our prayers through the wall?"

"I guess."

"Even if there's a really loud storm?"

"Sure, I guess."

I wait to see if he has any more questions, but he's quiet again.

Between worrying about Jake and waiting for Mom to call, I thought I'd never fall asleep. But I must have, because a really loud clap of thunder wakes me up. Freddy's probably scared.

"Hey, Freddy. You awake?"

There's another gigantic thunderclap, right over our heads. It's so loud it even scares *me*. No way he can sleep through that.

"Freddy? You okay?"

I jump down to check on him, but he's not there. Neither is Pita.

"Freddy?" I look under his bed, then grab my flashlight and head down the hall, calling his name softly so I don't wake anyone.

I check the bathroom, living room, kitchen . . . then I see it. The door to the carport is open just a bit. Just enough to let me know Freddy's not in the house—at all.

CHAPTER THIRTY-ONE

I grab the first two raincoats I see hanging in the hall closet and head out through the carport.

"FREDDY! WHERE ARE YOU?" I scream into the storm. I race around outside the Todds' house shouting until my throat hurts. It's cold and pouring and pitch-black everywhere I look. I'm drenched and shivering and I've only been outside a few minutes.

Freddy's gone.

I decide to count to one hundred. If I don't find him by then, I'm getting the Todds.

I'm up to thirty-seven when I get another idea. I run across the street to our house, shining my light in every direction.

And there's my little brother, standing under our carport. Lips moving, eyes closed, hands wrapped around Pita Rabbit.

"FREDDY!" I sprint toward him as lightning zigzags overhead.

"God? Is that you?"

"It's me, you idiot!" I shout over the thunder.

"Ethan? What are you doing out here?"

I wrap his shivering, skinny body in a wet raincoat. "What do you think I'm doing? Let's go!"

I take his cold, clammy hand and we run across the street together.

I grab a couple of towels and we dry off the best we can. As we peel off our wet clothes and slip into dry ones, part of me wants to yell at him for running out in the storm. But the bigger part is just relieved and grateful that he's okay. Still, I can't help saying, "Freddy, you can't run out like that. It's the middle of the night! And there's thunder and lightning and I woke up and you weren't here and . . ."

"Sorry," he says. "Are you mad at me?"

He looks so pitiful. His hair is soaking wet; even his eyelashes are dripping.

"No," I admit. "I'm not mad at you. But it still doesn't mean—"

"Do you think God heard me?" Freddy asks.

I hesitate. I don't want to say the wrong thing. So I go for the truth, and tell him, "I hope so."

He wraps his skinny arms around me and I hug him back, then we crawl into our bunk beds. I pull the blanket over my head, but it's impossible to go back to sleep. All I can think about is Jake.

Did he make it through the storm?

* * * * * * * * * * * * * * * * * *

Breakfast is surreal. I'm so tired I can't even pour milk in my cereal without spilling it on the table. "Sorry." I reach across for napkins and almost knock over my orange juice.

"I've got it." Mrs. Todd sops up the milk with paper towels.

"That was some storm last night," Chris says. "I thought the roof was going to cave in!"

"Did you two get any sleep?" Mr. Todd asks Freddy and me as he takes his coffee cup to the sink.

Freddy opens his big cereal-filled mouth, sure to get us in trouble, but I beat him to it.

"A little," I say.

As I try to finish breakfast without falling asleep in my cereal bowl, Mr. Todd walks back into the kitchen, carrying a wet raincoat.

"Anybody know anything about this?"

Uh-oh. I was so glad Freddy was okay and we were out of the rain, I threw the coats straight into the closet and forgot about them.

Freddy stops chewing and looks at me, the guilt on his face so clear a jury would convict him in a heartbeat. The Todds look at me, too: four pairs of eyes staring; four pairs of ears waiting to see what I come up with.

I do what I always do when I'm about to get in trouble: change the subject. "Did my mom ever call last night?"

Sure enough, it works. After a few seconds of silence, Mrs. Todd says, "You know, it's possible she couldn't get through because of the storm."

"That's a good point," Mr. Todd agrees. "But it still doesn't explain these wet coats." He raises his eyebrows in my direction.

"It's my fault," Freddy says. "I—"

"We left Pita Rabbit at our house," I say. I know it's not the truth, but it's less complicated. I look at Freddy, wondering if he'll go along. He looks at me, too. Then he looks at Mr. Todd.

"Sorry about the coats," Freddy says.

He smiles at Freddy. "That's okay. They'll dry."

"Next time," Chris adds, "take an umbrella."

At school, I have the weirdest sensation, like there's this layer of glass between me and everyone else. I see my teachers' worried expressions through it and hear my friends' voices, but nothing touches me.

I'm staring at my blank math quiz, wondering why

decimals were invented, when there's a knock at the door. Miss Wright answers, speaks with another teacher, and then makes a beeline toward my desk.

"Ethan," she whispers, "your parents are here. Please pack up and go to the front office."

My heart starts pounding and I feel sick to my stomach. I shut my binder, grab my backpack and leave the room, feeling like a robot. Before reaching the office, I stop by the band room and pick up my trumpet. Then I stop at a water fountain, even though I'm not thirsty, and take as long a drink as I can to put off seeing Mom and Dad. Put off hearing what they couldn't say last night.

Some things you just can't say over the phone.

I feel like I'm at the doctor's office waiting to get a shot. I want someone else to do this instead of me. Only the one who always goes first isn't here.

I have to be brave like Jake.

I take a deep breath, let it out in one big *whoosh*, then put one foot in front of the other and head to the front office.

Before I'm halfway there, Mom is in the hallway running toward me.

My legs turn to spaghetti and I slide down to the floor and shut my eyes. Maybe this is all a nightmare and if I keep my eyes closed long enough . . .

"Sweetie? Are you okay?" I feel her hand on my shoulder. "Ethan..."

I open my eyes.

She's smiling, not crying. "Jake took a huge turn last night. The doctors couldn't believe it!" She's hugging me now, laughing and crying. Then Dad's there, too, hugging and laughing and crying. And so am I.

"The doctors are calling Jake 'The Miracle Baby.'" Mom eases out of the hug and pulls some tissues from her pocket for all of us.

"He was touch and go all night but all of a sudden..." Dad breaks off, unable to finish his sentence. Mom touches his hand and starts tearing up again. Dad lets out a breath, then puts one arm around her shoulder and the other around mine. "Should we go tell Freddy the good news?"

On the ride home, Freddy asks a thousand questions, and our parents do their best to answer: Jake is doing a lot better; they don't know when he'll come home yet; Mom's going to spend days with him and nights with us; and we can see him later this week.

Once we get home, Mom makes a zillion phone calls while I help Dad collect the laundry. I grab a pair of jeans from my closet and toss it on top of the other clothes on my bed. I'm about to carry everything downstairs when I remember something. I search through the pockets and find red crinkly paper in one and a fortune cookie message in the other. I unfold the small white paper and read my fortune: "The greatest gift of all is one you already have."

"Ethan, my prayers worked! I saved Jakey!" Freddy barges in and plops down on my bed, even though it's covered with dirty laundry.

Is Jake alive because God answered Freddy's prayers? Does that mean if Freddy hadn't prayed, God wouldn't have saved him? Or what if Freddy hadn't prayed, but I had? Would God still have saved Jake?

"I'm going to start praying every night," Freddy announces. "Do you think, if I pray hard enough, God will let me get a really expensive Star Wars Lego?"

I throw my pillow at him. "It doesn't work like that. You don't just pray for something and get it."

"How do you know?" he asks.

"Because everyone would get everything they want all the time."

"What's wrong with that?"

"It doesn't work that way. What about all the poor people? Or the hungry people?" Or all the sick people who *don't* get better?

Freddy-the-Philosopher shrugs.

"What about Jake?" I ask.

"What about him? He's gonna be okay."

"Why wasn't he okay in the first place? Why did he come home with an oxygen tank and NG tube and all that other stuff? Why can't he walk and talk and eat like we do?"

"Maybe no one prayed hard enough," Freddy says.

"That's dumb."

"So you explain it," he says.

I think about it, off and on, all night. And I can't.

CHAPTER THIRTY-TWO

Next day, after school, I linger in my English classroom, hoping Ms. Carlin and I can talk for a bit. Sure enough, she tells me to grab a seat, then takes a chocolate bar from her desk drawer and joins me. She hands me the bigger half, then says, "It's been quite a rollercoaster for your family, hasn't it?"

I nod. "We weren't sure Jake was gonna make it, but he pulled through."

Ms. Carlin smiles. "That's wonderful, Ethan."

I nod again. "Freddy went out in the storm to pray. The next day, Jake was better. Freddy says it's because God answered his prayers. . . . Do you think he's right?"

"What do *you* think?" She smiles, using one of those annoying tricks they learn at teacher school.

I don't smile back. "If God answers our prayers, why was Jake hurt in the first place?"

"Excellent question."

I wait for an excellent answer. It doesn't come.

Ms. Carlin looks at me for what feels like forever, then says, "Maybe you need to ask a different question."

"Like what?"

"Instead of asking why Jake is hurt, maybe think about why Jake is *here*."

I close my eyes and picture him in my mind. I see him so clearly, gulping down his bottle, shaking his jingle sticks, smiling. Jake makes more out of the little he has than some people make out of a whole lot more.

All this time I thought I was helping Jake, but *he's* been helping me, too. He helps me keep trying when it's easier to give up. He shows me that even little things can be huge and can make people happy. And he helps me believe in myself—makes me feel like I can do anything. And like anything I do is the greatest thing ever.

I think of the definition for magic I used in my report on Magnus the Magnificent: "any mysterious, seemingly inexplicable, or extraordinary power or influence."

Suddenly—finally—I see what I should have all along: Jake is the real magician in our family.

● ● ● ● ● ● ● ● ● ● ● ● ● ● ● ● ● ●

It's been a week since "The Miracle Baby" pulled off the best magic trick of all, and today he's finally coming home again.

I'm in such a good mood, I don't even mind going to school. When I get to the corner, Betty is there like always, blowing her whistle in the freezing cold. "Hey, Ethan, how's it goin'?"

"Better," I tell her. "Much better."

In band, I reach the highest note I've ever played and Daniel and Brian give me high fives. I manage to remember all my French vocabulary, and when I get to math class, I raise my hand when Miss Wright asks who can answer question seven in our homework. I even get the answer right.

It's not like I love math all of a sudden; I've just decided to start trying my best . . . like someone else I know.

"When's Jakey gonna be here?" Freddy asks for the thousandth time.

And, for the thousandth time, Emma looks up from the latch hook rug she's making and says, "Soon, sweetheart. Soon."

Satisfied for the moment, Freddy searches for the next piece to his jigsaw puzzle. Bubba brings another cup of tea to Emma, and I get back to *The Fires of Merlin*. I'm rereading the chapter where Merlin is trapped in the stone and can't move or talk or anything. It's one of my favorite parts of the whole book, but it's hard to focus.

We're all pretending to be busy, but what we're really doing is waiting for Jake.

I think of the first time he came home from the hospital, when he was just a baby. I remember the blue minivan pulling into the carport, and my grandparents all teary-eyed and Freddy jumping up and down. I remember Dad carrying Jake toward us, and Mom saying, "Jake's home."

Most of all, I remember touching Jake's face and putting my finger in his teeny hand, and how he held on really tight, like he would never let go.

After what seems like forever, the same blue minivan finally pulls into our driveway.

"They're here!" Freddy shouts. He races to the door, with me right behind.

And everybody's smiling and hugging and we're all together and it's magic.

Jake is home.

———————————

It's one o'clock in the morning. I'm wide awake, staring at the glow-in-the-dark stars on the ceiling. My thoughts are racing, but my body is still. My nose itches, but I don't scratch it. My right leg is stiff, and I have a crick in my neck, but I don't move, not even a fraction of an inch. I barely even blink.

I am stone, like Merlin.

I am trapped, like Jake.

There are so many things he'll probably never do, but he smiles anyway—even all those times I let him down and don't stretch him.

Even when I said I did . . . but I didn't.

Tears slide down my cheeks. I don't move a muscle to wipe them. Words ricochet in the dark without being spoken: *I'm sorry, Jake. So sorry.*

A few more minutes go by. Then I crawl out of bed, open my door, and cross the hall. I enter Jake's room quietly, in case he's asleep, and gently sit down on his little bed. There's just enough light from the Tweety Bird night-light for me to see a pair of blue eyes looking at me expectantly.

"Hey, Jake. I know it's late, but I couldn't sleep. Guess you couldn't, either." I pull him toward me and hug him close, then put him on his rainbow-colored quilt and bring his hands together. "I'm really sorry about all those times I didn't stretch you. I promise I'll do better from now on, okay?"

He smiles as always, and I know he's forgiven me. Even if I don't deserve it.

I squeeze his hands again, then move his stiff arms up and down and in and out and up and down and in and out. . . .

CHAPTER THIRTY-THREE

Since Jake is back home, Mom and I have time to work on the fund-raiser again; it's only a couple weeks away now. Luckily, a lot got done without us. Like Tina told me, she lined up the high school jazz band and show choir, plus got a bunch of local restaurants to donate food and gift certificates for that night. Katie's mom made flyers and put together a silent auction. And Peter's mom teamed up with C.K.'s to research playground equipment.

Mom and I are at the kitchen table looking through a big catalog Peter's mom gave us. "Look at this one." Mom grabs her pen and jots the name and price on a piece of paper. "It's called a 'cozy cocoon.' Everyone can use it, but it's designed especially for autistic children, like C.K." She shows me this circular, mostly-enclosed space that's open in front and has round openings for windows.

"How would it help him?"

She takes a sip of mint tea. "You know how he gets upset sometimes when there's too much noise? This is a quiet space where he could calm down and feel safe until he's ready to play again."

Anything that'll calm C.K. down sounds good to me.

She flips to the next page that's flagged when my new cell phone rings. The day after Jake came home, Mom and Dad surprised me with it. They said I'd done such a great job taking care of Freddy and "holding down the fort," that I earned it.

"It's Amazing Amelia," I tell Mom.

"You go ahead. I'll check on your brothers." She takes her mug and leaves.

Amazing Amelia has been texting me every week. The first time, she wanted to know how Jake was doing, and to be sure he was okay. It wasn't until we were ready to say goodbye that I remembered to ask who won the magic competition.

"Oh," she typed. "I did."

Before I could even congratulate her, she added, "But we'll never know what would've happened if you had stayed."

Nope. We never will.

I'm happy for her. I really am. But every time I hear from her, I can't help wondering what would've happened if I *had* stayed. Would she still have won?

"Ethan?" she texts.

"I'm here. So, are you and Magnus partners yet?" I ask, like always.

And like always, she sends a smiley face. "Not yet." Only this time she adds, "But I'm going to meet him soon. And I want you to be one of my guests. Afterward, you can meet him if you want."

If I *want*? "That would be awesome! You really *are* amazing."

We end the conversation a few minutes later, but I can't stop smiling.

"That must've been quite a conversation." Mom walks back into the kitchen.

"I'm going to meet Magnus after all! Amelia just invited me to the show!"

"I'm so happy for you, Ethan." She gives me a hug, then sits at the table and gets her pen again. "Give me all the details."

"Okay. Well, the ticket is free, plus Amelia's aunt and uncle live in D.C., so I can ride up to Atlantic City with them if you want. She gave me their number if you'd like to talk with them."

"Sounds like she's thought of everything. Now, what's the date?"

"February twelfth." I want to jump up and down like

Freddy when he's super excited. I want to fly around the room, and—

"Oh," Mom says.

One word is all it takes for my excitement to come crashing down. Something is wrong, I just can't figure out what. . . . Then I realize. "That's when the fund-raiser is."

She nods. I look at her. She looks at me. I know what she's thinking.

"Listen," I tell her. "It's not like I don't want to be at the fund-raiser, but this is Magnus we're talking about! I've wanted to meet him since forever and I thought I couldn't and now I can and—"

"You're right." She reaches across the table and takes my hand.

"Wait, what?"

"You deserve this, Ethan. You should go."

The doorbell rings before either of us can say anything else. Mom opens the door, and I hear her say, "Well, hello, Katie. You look very stylish."

"I know," Katie says. "Is Ethan here?"

Next thing I know she's spinning around in front of me. "Ethan? What do you think? Do you like my outfit?" She's wearing a sparkly top hat and bowtie, both purple. "I got them for our magic act!"

I don't know what to say. Don't know how to tell her there won't *be* a magic act, because I won't be at the fund-raiser.

A week ago, I came up with the idea of having her and Peter in my act—along with Freddy—because the whole point of the fund-raiser is to include everyone. Besides, after my magic prop meltdown, it seemed like a good time for new tricks, and new assistants.

Katie twirls around again. She looks so happy, I can't tell her I'll be somewhere else. Instead, I say, "You look great."

She hugs me. "See ya tomorrow!" And she runs back out the door.

Tomorrow: another rehearsal with her and Peter and Freddy.

I look at Mom again and she looks at me again and neither of us looks very happy. "You're going to have to tell her. And Peter," she says. "Freddy too."

"Tell me what?" Freddy runs into the living room.

I put on a really big, really fake smile. "I'm finally going to meet Magnus."

"You are?" He smiles back at me. "When?"

"The same night as the fund-raiser."

Freddy's eyebrows practically meet. "You're gonna do both?"

"Um . . . actually, I'm only going to see Magnus."

Mom touches my shoulder. "I need to check on Jake." She walks down the hall, leaving me alone with Freddy, who looks like I just destroyed his entire Lego collection.

"But what about our new act?" he stammers.

"I already gave up the chance to meet Magnus once. Even Mom says I shouldn't have to do it again."

His face collapses. He doesn't say anything, just stands there, staring at me.

"Besides, the new act probably isn't that great anyway. It's not the same without my props and everything," I say, trying to make him feel better.

A weird expression comes over his face and then he runs down the hall. I guess he's more upset than I realized.

A minute later he's back, lugging a huge, bulging plastic bag behind him.

My bag. "Here." He hands it to me. I open it and, sure enough, all my magic supplies are there.

"I threw this away."

"I know," he says. "I unthrowed it."

I look through, piece by piece, but still can't believe it. Can't believe he kept it. "Freddy, why did you . . . ?"

He looks at me and smiles. "'Cause everybody needs magic," he says, like it's the most obvious thing in the world.

And maybe it is.

It's past midnight, but I can't sleep.

All I want is to meet Magnus.

And to perform at the fund-raiser.

What I want is impossible.

I decide if anyone knows about doing the impossible, it's Jake. I go to his room as quietly as I can. His blue eyes are open, and I can tell he's happy to see me, like always. I close his door, sit on his little toddler bed, and pull him into my lap.

"Hey, Jake. Can you believe I finally get to meet Magnus? How cool is that? Much cooler than performing with Freddy and Peter and Katie at the fund-raiser, right?" I squeeze his hands and move them back and forth super fast, the way he likes. Only he isn't smiling the way he usually does.

It's probably just my imagination.

I feel his forehead like Mom does, in case he's sick again, but he doesn't feel hot or anything.

"You're not worried, are you, Jake? We're still gonna get that equipment for the playground. People already bought lots of tickets, so we've got the money even if I don't show up."

For the millionth time, I imagine myself with Magnus. We're behind stage, and he says Amazing Amelia told him all about me. He asks me to show him one of my tricks, and I do, and he loves it. He smiles and shakes my hand and says maybe someday we'll perform together.

Then I picture myself onstage with Katie in her purple top hat and Peter in his wheelchair. I see Freddy jumping up and down with excitement, and the rest of my family in the front row. And I see Jake, smiling up at me.

I picture myself with Magnus again, but it doesn't feel the same.

I don't feel the same.

"Hey, Jake . . ." I bend down my head and whisper into his ear, then squeeze his hands together and move them back and forth, just like I did before.

This time, he grins like it's the best thing ever.

CHAPTER THIRTY-FOUR

When my family and I walk into the high school auditorium, it's already packed. People I don't even know are smiling at me. And people I know, too, like Chris and his parents, Tina, Rox, Wendy and Ned, and even Ms. Carlin, who waves as I walk down the aisle.

The jazz band is fantastic, and the show choir's good enough to go on one of those reality talent shows and take first place.

Then it's our turn to perform. Freddy joins me onstage in his usual magician's assistant outfit. He bows to the audience until I say, "That's enough for now." I fan a deck of cards in front of him. "Pick a card, any card."

He does, then turns to the audience and, in the loudest voice he can muster, shouts, "The queen of clubs!"

I roll my eyes in disgust. "Don't say it out loud!"

"Oops."

The audience chuckles.

"All right, try it again. This time don't tell them what card you have, just show them."

Freddy frowns. "I don't think they'll be able to see the card in the back row."

"We can help with that." Katie skips onto the stage from the side door, wearing a black tux along with the purple bowtie and top hat. Peter, wearing a green bowtie and top hat, pushes a button on his wheelchair and comes in right after her, riding over to center stage. In his lap, he's holding a huge, glittery top hat Tina made out of cardboard for tonight's show.

Katie helps Peter pull out typical magic props, like colorful silk scarves tied together and a big white rabbit (stuffed, not real).

Then she pulls out a banana.

Freddy's eyes grow wide. "Can I have that? Being a guest magician makes me hungry!" He peels it and starts eating. Then Peter pulls out a sandwich, which Katie grabs, unwraps, and bites into. Next is a ginormous chocolate bar.

"Hey!" I cry. "This isn't a picnic! We're supposed to be doing a card trick here."

"Oops," Freddy says. The audience is really into it now, laughing and shouting encouragement—especially to Peter and Katie, who are grinning like crazy.

I give a very dramatic sigh. "I guess you get what you pay for."

"You didn't pay us anything," Katie points out.

"Exactly," I tell the audience.

Finally, Katie helps Peter pull a long, rolled-up sheet of paper out of the top hat, and Freddy finds a thick red marker.

I fan out the cards again and Freddy picks one, writes something on the paper, and shows the audience.

"Okay," I tell him, "now put the card back into the deck."

He does, just as Katie runs up and hugs me.

"I love magic," she says.

"Doesn't everyone?" I ask. The crowd cheers. Katie hugs Freddy, then runs over and hugs Peter, too.

"All right. Time to reveal your card. Is it...the ace of spades?"

Freddy looks nervous and shakes his head. I hear a few disappointed groans from the crowd.

"Okay. Hold on . . . is it the ace of diamonds?"

He shakes his head again. "This worked a lot better at home," Freddy tells the audience.

I take a deep breath and flip through the deck again. "I've got it. It's the ace of clubs."

Freddy slaps his forehead, like he can't believe this is happening. I turn to the audience. "Um, sorry about this. Can we start again?"

"Wait!" Katie pulls a card out of the big top hat. "Is it the ace of hearts?"

Freddy holds up the paper, which reveals an ace with a big heart underneath in red magic marker.

The crowd bursts into applause, and the four of us bow in unison.

As I thank Peter, Katie, and Freddy by name, each of them waves or takes a bow, then they leave the stage to join their families in the audience. I'm about to give Daniel the nod to start my King of Chaos music when I hear this voice somewhere in the auditorium. A voice I've heard on YouTube videos and TV specials, but never in person. A voice asking, "Might there be a spot for one more guest magician?"

I must be dreaming, or hallucinating. He's in Atlantic City, doing a show with Amelia. Is someone pulling a practical joke? Maybe it's some sort of recording to wish me luck. . . .

Then I see him, with his long hair and silver tux, walking down the center aisle toward the stage. Toward me.

I can't talk. Can't think. Can't. Even. Breathe.

All I can do is watch along with everyone else in the theater. A wave of excitement spreads through the crowd. People point and take pictures. Ms. Carlin fans her pink cheeks.

On his way to the stage, he stops by the front row and says

hi to Jake while Freddy jumps up and down, a super-sized smile on his face.

And then Magnus the Magnificent is onstage. Next to me. Just like I'd imagined so many times. Only this time, it's real. It must be, because I feel like I'm going to pass out.

He motions to the microphone. "May I say something?"

I nod, unable to form an intelligent thought let alone a sentence.

"A lovely young magician named Amazing Amelia invited Ethan to my show tonight in Atlantic City." He gives one of those dramatic pauses he's famous for. "Instead, he chose to come here." He turns to look at me. "It's not often someone stands me up. This could cause considerable damage to my reputation."

The audience laughs.

"Naturally, I was rather curious about his decision. After all, what could possibly be more gratifying than meeting me?" He smiles and the audience laughs again.

"Then Amelia told me about this fund-raiser. This wonderful fund-raiser that is, in fact, far more gratifying than meeting me. And I understood why my friend here wanted to be part of it."

Did Magnus the Magnificent just call me his friend?

"And I decided I wanted to be part of it as well."

The audience applauds.

Magnus smiles, then turns to me. "Shall we make some magic together, Ethan?"

"What about your show?" I ask, finally able to get a few words out.

"Not to worry. I've got a small jet waiting to fly me there." He turns to the audience. "A bit extravagant, I know. Still, there are times it proves rather useful, particularly when it's for a good cause." He winks, then turns to me again. "Now, before we get started, is there a Jake Miller in the audience?"

"He's right here!" Freddy shouts.

"Excellent," Magnus says. "Could you please see if he's holding a gold envelope?"

Freddy checks. "He is!"

"Would you be so kind as to bring it here?"

Freddy hugs Jake, grabs the envelope, and races up to the stage. Magnus thanks him and hands the envelope to me. "Please. Open it."

My fingers tremble, but I finally get it open. There's a piece of paper inside. I pull it out. "It's a check," I tell the audience. "For ten thousand dollars!"

The audience whoops and whistles and goes crazy, and it feels like the whole room is vibrating.

"I hope that might buy a piece or two for that beautiful

playground of yours," Magnus says.

"Thank you so much!" I feel like hugging him, but how uncool would that be? I settle for grinning like an idiot.

He gives one of his classy, trademark bows from the waist, then waits a few seconds for the crowd to calm down before speaking again.

"As you may appreciate, Ethan and I haven't had the opportunity to prepare, so if you good folks would kindly give us a few moments backstage to confer and conspire, we'll try to put something together. In the meantime, perhaps you might consider revisiting the lobby. I may have brought a few things with me. All proceeds will go toward purchasing more playground equipment."

The second the last syllable leaves his mouth, half the crowd rushes toward the aisles, including Freddy and Ms. Carlin.

I'm still feeling shaky, but in a good way, and manage to get my feet to follow Magnus backstage. Suddenly, it's just the two of us, which makes it even more real, and way more awesome.

"Ethan, before we get to work, I want to tell you something." Magnus gives me a super-intense look. "I hope you will remember it always."

Like I could forget one single second of this night. Still, I nod.

"We magicians don't often get the respect we deserve.

People scoff and scorn, say what we do is all smoke and mirrors. Sleight-of-hand and misdirection." He smiles. "Well, usually it is."

I smile back.

Then his famous face gets serious again. "Nonetheless, every once in a while, if you're very fortunate, you get to be part of *real* magic. Like tonight."

"Like you being here?"

He smiles and shakes his head. "It's nothing to do with me. It's about you. You, and your family and friends and this glorious audience. This outpouring of generosity and laughter and love. Ethan, tonight is magic at its best."

I'm standing backstage with Magnus the Magnificent, at a total loss for words. After what seems like forever, I say the first thing that comes to mind: "I still can't believe you're here."

"It's my pleasure. In fact, it's really a bit selfish on my part. You see, it's not every day I get to meet a real-life hero." He reaches a hand out and I go to shake it, but he pulls me in for a quick hug instead.

"Now, for the first bit, we'll need a member of the audience. Is there someone special you'd like to call on?"

I think for a couple seconds and a smile spreads across my face. "Well, there is this teacher I have—she's kind of a fan. . . ."

WAIT—THERE'S MORE!

Remember when I said, "When someone does something really nice, they deserve to learn an awesome magic trick"?

Well, you did something nice by finishing this book. So Super Jake and I decided to say thanks by revealing not one, but five of the magic tricks you read about!

If you want to discover the super-awesome solutions, just turn the page.

AWESOME MAGIC TRICK NUMBER ONE (FROM CHAPTER THREE)

····· ♥ ·····

STUFF YOU'LL NEED (ALWAYS CHEAP, AND ALMOST ALWAYS AVAILABLE):

★ Nine (or any number of) *identical* note cards
★ A pen or pencil

SUPER-SECRET INSTRUCTIONS:

1. On one side of each note card, write the name of a different Marvel character (or something else fun, like a favorite ice cream flavor. Or—if you have to—something un-fun, like a Disney princess). Nine's a good number, but you can use any number you like. Be sure you can't see the writing through the paper!

2. Put the tiniest dot you can on the blank side of the card you want "chosen" last. It should be so tiny that no one will notice . . . *except you.*

3. Tell your friend (or annoying sibling) what to expect when the last card is revealed. (I told Freddy it would be Captain America. Spoiler alert: it was.)

4. Let your friend choose any two cards, but be sure *you* turn them over. If neither has the dot, turn over either one. (You can even let your friend do it whenever there's no dot on either.) If one *does* have the dot, turn over the *other*. To be magnificent like Magnus, move the cards after each selection and/or shuffle whichever two are picked. The faster you do it, the more magnificent the trick will be!

5. When only two cards are left, turn over the one *without* the dot. Then let your friend turn over the last one. Abracadabra! Pretty awesome, right?

AWESOME MAGIC TRICK
NUMBER TWO
(FROM CHAPTER TEN):

····· ♥ ·····

STUFF YOU'LL NEED (ALWAYS CHEAP, AND ALMOST ALWAYS AVAILABLE):

★ A jacket or a napkin (preferably cloth, not paper)
★ Sugar packets
★ A quarter (preferably someone else's)
★ A permanent marker

SUPER-SECRET INSTRUCTIONS:

Note: This trick is kind of "tricky." You need skill, sleight of hand, patience, and practice. But if you can pull it off, it's worth the work—your friend will be amazed for sure.

1. To start with, put a napkin or jacket across your lap. It's best if no one notices. Have your friend choose a sugar packet and then mark the quarter with his or her initial—or a smiley face or whatever—using the permanent marker. Put the coin and the packet side by side on the table.

2. Drop the sugar packet into your open hand. Then *pretend* to drop the quarter in after it. What you really do is sweep the coin off the table and into your lap (which is covered with the napkin, so the coin won't fall to the ground. Get it?).

3. As soon as you "drop" the coin into your hand, close it immediately! Your friend will *assume* the coin is with the packet.

4. Have your friend squeeze the hand that you have the sugar packet and (supposedly) coin in to "combine" both of these items. While they're squeezing your hand, pick up the coin from your lap with your other hand (hold it with your thumb and index finger, making sure to keep it hidden). Bring your hand back and let it rest on the table.

5. Tell them to let go of your hand; open it and put the packet on the table. Make a big production out of shaking the packet. Tell them the coin is inside.

6. Put the packet into the hand holding the coin. When you tear it open, the coin is under the packet. As you start to pour the sugar into your friend's hand, let the coin drop at the same time so it looks like it's falling out of the packet along with the sugar. How sweet is that?

AWESOME MAGIC TRICK NUMBER THREE (FROM CHAPTER SEVENTEEN)

••••• ♥ •••••

STUFF YOU'LL NEED (ALWAYS CHEAP, AND ALMOST ALWAYS AVAILABLE):

★ A deck of cards

★ You'll also need an assistant for this one who knows how the trick works, so plan ahead!

SUPER-SECRET INSTRUCTIONS:

1. Put ten cards on the table, faceup, *including the number ten*. You can use any number you like, but bigger is better—more cards for you, and your guest, to choose from.

2. Here's the important part: *whatever* number you choose, always include *a card that's the same number*. Like, if you use nine cards, be sure one of them *is* a nine. Get it? Otherwise, this trick will *not* be awesome.

3. Here's the other important part: put the cards down *in the same pattern as the symbols on the ten card.*

4. Have your friend/parent/teacher choose a card and whisper it to your partner.

5. Your partner points to one card at a time. The secret is to use the ten card to show you which card it is. If your partner doesn't point to the ten card right away (and they won't always), it's not the right one.

6. Once they *do* point to the ten card, they need to be very careful and point to *the location* of the right card by putting a finger where the card is in the ten pattern. That's how your partner shows you the right card! Get it? How cool is that?

AWESOME MAGIC TRICK
NUMBER FOUR
(ALSO FROM CHAPTER SEVENTEEN)

•••••♠•••••

STUFF YOU'LL NEED (ALWAYS CHEAP, AND ALMOST ALWAYS AVAILABLE):

★ Crayons

SUPER-SECRET INSTRUCTIONS:

1. Show your friend, grandparent, or (occasionally, but not always) annoying sibling some crayons. Let them choose one.

2. While your back is turned, have them place it in your right hand (if you're a lefty, like me) or your left, if you're right-handed.

3. Turn around but keep your hands behind your back long enough to scrape a tiny bit of crayon with the thumb that isn't holding the crayon.

4. Bring whichever hand has the crayon mark in front of your body and take a quick peek at it so you can see the color wax you've scraped off from the crayon. But you should look like you're thinking really hard (I find it helpful to channel

Freddy) to figure out the color. Feel free to go on about limes and grass if it's green, or school buses and bananas if it's yellow—you get the idea. This one's awesome *and* easy. If little brothers can do it, so can you!

AWESOME MAGIC TRICK
NUMBER FIVE
(FROM CHAPTER THIRTY)

•••• ♥ ••••

STUFF YOU'LL NEED (ALWAYS CHEAP, AND ALMOST ALWAYS AVAILABLE):

★ A deck of cards

SUPER-SECRET INSTRUCTIONS:

1. Have someone pick a card from the deck and show it to their friends.

2. As they are showing the card around, flip the bottom card of the deck, then turn the deck upside down.

3. Show them the deck faceup. (The flipped card makes it look like the deck is still facedown.)

4. Have them put their card in anywhere, facedown. Be sure to hold the cards tightly so they don't fan out and give the trick away!

5. Thumb through the deck until you find their card. (It will be the only other one facedown, since the rest are faceup.) This one's so easy that even annoying brothers can do it—but it's still awesome.

ACKNOWLEDGMENTS

So many people have helped me on my path to publication that it's hard to know where to start. So I'll start at the beginning. My parents, Freeda and Martin Wender, loved, supported, and believed in me so unquestioningly, I had no choice but to believe, too. Thanks also to my brother, Charles, for being there for me, and for all things Jake-related.

Two other people believed in me, too; without them, this book would not be in your hands. My amazing and awesome agent, Liza Fleissig, whose passion, and compassion, are without equal; and my incredible and incomparable editor, Julie Matysik, who championed this book, and whose guidance, care, and meticulous editing made our collaboration a joy and a privilege. I am beyond grateful to them both, as well as the Running Press Kids team: project editor Michael Clark, copy editor Susan Hom, marketing and publicity manager Valerie

Howlett, junior designer Christopher Eads, illustrator Erwin Madrid, and publisher Kristin Kiser.

I wouldn't be here without the help and support of my long-running critique group family, past and present, especially Betty May, Cecily Nabors, Diana Belchase, Lesley Moore Vossen, Liz Sues, Miriam Chernick, Penny March, and Sarah Swan. Their feedback, and friendship, is invaluable.

I am so fortunate to have three more extraordinary writers in my life and in my corner: Marissa Moss, Laura Shovan, and my Pitch Wars mentor, Veronica Bartles. They all helped me navigate uncharted territory with never-ending patience and overwhelming generosity.

I want to thank Esther Hershenhorn, whose gentle suggestions pointed me in the right direction early on, and whose enthusiasm and kindness have continued right up to the end. And I want to give (at least) three cheers for the one and only Brenda Drake, who created Pitch Wars and all its awesomeness. Thank you, Brenda, for the endless opportunities Pitch Wars creates for so many writers. We owe you a tremendous debt.

Anyone who knows anything about children's book writers and illustrators knows that these acknowledgments would be incomplete without paying tribute to Lin Oliver, Stephen Mooser, and everyone else who puts their time, energy, and love into the phenomenal organization known as SCBWI. Your impact is immeasurable.

Thanks to Linda, John, and Todd Culbertson, for their involvement in Jake's life and their continuing friendship. I hereby nominate all three of them for sainthood. Special thanks to Pam and Kristina Ackley, for their boundless devotion to Jake and their integral part, and continuing involvement, in Jake's Garden. It gives me great pleasure and pride to know that, because of her time with Jake, Kristina has dedicated her life to helping children with special needs.

I have to thank Rosa Hsiung, my long-suffering best friend, cheerleader, and confidante. After all these years, she deserves her own paragraph. I owe her more than I can express in one sentence (plus an infinite supply of hot beverages).

I want to thank Lee Milliner for being the best husband, and dad, I could hope for. And I give my deepest thanks to Jake's big brothers, Jeremy and Jesse. Jeremy's humor and creativity, and Jesse's unconditional love and playfulness, made Jake's life a very happy one.

I should also thank Jeremy for coming up with at least two of my favorite lines, which have beaten the odds and made it to the final draft! And an extra heaping of love and gratitude to Jesse for his tireless efforts and unwavering faith, both in this book and in me. Words are not enough.

Last and most of all, I thank Jake for his sweetness and his fighting spirit. He inspires me still to keep trying no matter what, and to never give up. That, more than anything, is why this book is here.

I love you, Jake.

A TRIBUTE TO JAKE: ONE BROTHER TO ANOTHER

On May 6, 2007, Jake's family and friends gathered together to celebrate the opening of Jake's Garden, then housed at our local library. We chose to incorporate two themes in his garden. The first was *Goodnight Moon* by Margaret Wise Brown. This was Jake's favorite book, and his brother Jesse read it to him often. The other theme was butterflies, because Jake was so like a butterfly—beautiful and ephemeral. Both of these themes were represented by mosaics created by Jake's babysitter, Kristina Ackley (Tina in the book), and her mother, Pamela Ackley.

The dedication was filled with music and laughter and tears—and a very special butterfly release. Poetry was read, memories were shared, and speeches were given.

My favorite speech of all was written and delivered by my oldest son—and Jake's brother—Jeremy, who was sixteen at the time. He said it was "okay" for me to share it with you:

"Since Jake was born, he was called a 'fighter' . . . whether it was against waking up in time for a therapy session or refusing to choke down the dreaded Poly-Vi-Sol. But most of the time, Jake's considered a fighter because he rose above his disability; because he overcame the obstacles that were stacked against him.

"This is no doubt true, but let me tell you a lesser-known account of Jake's fighting ability. Jake wasn't exactly legendary for his wrestling skills—but he should have been. We wrestled on the sofa, and he won every time: weight and drool can be a deadly combination.

"One of the synonyms for *fighter* is *champion*. And if that's not Jake, nothing is."